A native of Poland, **Joseph Conrad** (1857–1924) spent his youth at sea, and although relatively ignorant of the English language until the age of twenty, he ultimately became one of the greatest of English novelists and stylists. At the age of thirty-two, he decided to try his hand at writing, left the sea, married, and became the father of two sons. Although his work won the admiration of critics, sales were small, and debts and poor health plagued Conrad for many years. He was a nervous, introverted, gloomy man for whom writing was an agony, but he was rich in friends who appreciated his genius, among them Henry James, Stephen Crane, and Ford Madox Ford. Among his best-known works are *Almayer's Folly* (1895), *The Nigger of the "Narcissus"* (1897), *Lord Jim* (1900), *Heart of Darkness* (1902), *The Secret Agent* (1907), *Chance* (1913), and *Victory* (1915).

Joyce Carol Oates is the author of numerous novels, as well as collections of stories, poetry, and plays. The Roger S. Berlind Distinguished Professor in the Humanities at Princeton University, she is the recipient of numerous literary awards, including the National Book Award, the PEN–Bernard Malamud Award for the short story, and the Prix Femina.

Vince Passaro is the author of *Violence, Nudity, Adult Content: A Novel,* as well as criticism, essays, and short fiction that have appeared in many national magazines, including *Harper's, Esquire, GQ, Elle, O The Oprah Magazine, The New York Times Sunday Magazine, Story, Open City,* Salon.com, and others. Both his fiction and essays have been widely anthologized, and he has taught literature and creative writing at New York University and Columbia University.

JOSEPH CONRAD

Heart of Darkness
and
The Secret Sharer

With an Introduction by
JOYCE CAROL OATES
and a New Afterword by
VINCE PASSARO

SIGNET CLASSICS

SIGNET CLASSICS
Published by New American Library, a division of
Penguin Group (USA) Inc., 375 Hudson Street,
New York, New York 10014, USA
Penguin Group (Canada), 90 Eglinton Avenue East, Suite 700, Toronto,
Ontario M4P 2Y3, Canada (a division of Pearson Penguin Canada Inc.)
Penguin Books Ltd., 80 Strand, London WC2R 0RL, England
Penguin Ireland, 25 St. Stephen's Green, Dublin 2,
Ireland (a division of Penguin Books Ltd.)
Penguin Group (Australia), 250 Camberwell Road, Camberwell, Victoria 3124,
Australia (a division of Pearson Australia Group Pty. Ltd.)
Penguin Books India Pvt. Ltd., 11 Community Centre, Panchsheel Park,
New Delhi - 110 017, India
Penguin Group (NZ), 67 Apollo Drive, Rosedale, North Shore 0632,
New Zealand (a division of Pearson New Zealand Ltd.)
Penguin Books (South Africa) (Pty.) Ltd., 24 Sturdee Avenue,
Rosebank, Johannesburg 2196, South Africa

Penguin Books Ltd., Registered Offices:
80 Strand, London WC2R 0RL, England

Published by Signet Classics, an imprint of New American Library,
a division of Penguin Group (USA) Inc.

First Signet Classics Printing, December 1950
First Signet Classics Printing (Passaro Afterword), August 2008
10 9 8 7

Introduction copyright © The Ontario Review, Inc., 1997
Afterword copyright © Vince Passaro, 2008
All rights reserved

 REGISTERED TRADEMARK—MARCA REGISTRADA

Printed in the United States of America

Contents

Introduction

> My task which I am trying to achieve is, by the
> power of the written word, to make you hear, to
> make you feel—it is, before all, to make you *see.*
> —Joseph Conrad,
>   Preface, *The Nigger of the "Narcissus,"*
>   1897

Like those other masterworks of the English fin de
siècle, Robert Louis Stevenson's *Dr. Jekyll and Mr.
Hyde* (1886), Oscar Wilde's *The Picture of Dorian
Gray* (1890–91), and Henry James's *The Turn of the
Screw* (1898), to which it bears a subtle thematic kinship, Joseph Conrad's "Heart of Darkness" (1902) is a
work of the imagination that has transcended its late-
Victorian era to acquire the stature, with the passing of
time, of one of the great visionary self-examinations of
Western civilization. Based, like most of Conrad's fiction, upon personal experience, "Heart of Darkness" is
a rare Symbolist work with roots in historic authenticity;
its theme is nothing less than the acknowledgment of a
tragic darkness—the ethic of the "brute"—in the heart
of late-nineteenth-century Christian-capitalist Europe.
Out of his outraged witnessing of what he called "the
vilest scramble for loot that ever disfigured the history
of human consciousness"—the plunder of Africa by
Europe—Conrad created a universal parable of man's
fallen nature in the guise of an adventure/mystery tale.

In *Dr. Jekyll and Mr. Hyde,* Robert Louis Stevenson created a vivid, iconic metaphor for civilized man's divided nature: there is the "good" if passionless Dr. Jekyll, and there is his suppressed brother self, the stunted, impassioned, "evil" Hyde who dwells within Jekyll and can be released—fatally—by a magic elixir. In Oscar Wilde's *The Picture of Dorian Gray,* the seductively beautiful young Dorian commits sins against humanity that are engraved, not on his unblemished, never-aging face, but on the face of his portrait, which has been hidden away: what more striking metaphor for the hypocritical nature of privileged Caucasian bourgeois society? In Henry James's enigmatic *The Turn of the Screw,* that most elegantly constructed of ghost stories, the reader is confronted by a seemingly good Christian governess who may herself be the catalyst of the destruction of her young charges: Does this zealous, well-intentioned young woman discover perversity and evil surrounding her, or is she luridly imagining it? Joseph Conrad's "Heart of Darkness," though elaborately composed of oscillating images of light and dark, order and chaos, is by far the most realistic of these unusual works of fiction; yet here, too, is a powerful mythic portrait of a "good" man, Kurtz (the chief of the inner station of the trading company, "an emissary of pity, and science, and progress, and devil knows what else"), who is simultaneously an "evil" man (a vicious, unscrupulous trader in ivory who ends up tyrannizing African natives, his jungle sanctuary surrounded by the grisly emblems of his madness, the decapitated heads of native "enemies"). Kurtz, whom Marlow had sought avidly, risking his own life in a treacherous and foolhardy adventure that comes close to destroying him, is both Dr. Jekyll and Mr. Hyde; the elixir that fatally releases his primitive, evil self is simply distance from home, the freedom of a white man's power over those whom he considers his racial "inferiors," whose influence over him is subliminal and unacknowledged:

I tried to break the spell [Marlow says]—the heavy, mute spell of the wilderness—that seemed to draw him to its pitiless breast by the awakening of forgotten and brutal instincts, by the memory of gratified and monstrous passions. This alone, I was convinced, had driven him out to the edge of the forest, to the bush, towards the gleam of fires, the throb of drums, the drone of weird incantations. . . . There was nothing either above or below him, and I knew it. He had kicked himself loose of the earth. . . . [H]is soul was mad. Being alone in the wilderness, it had looked within itself, and, by heavens! I tell you, it had gone mad.

It is Marlow's compelling argument, and through Marlow, Conrad's, that the mind of man is capable of anything "because everything is in it, all the past as well as all the future." Marlow's (and Conrad's) journey up the Congo is, in one sense, a journey back into time: beginning with Marlow's apprehension that England, too, was once "one of the dark places of the earth" and moving to a consideration of the "fascination of the abomination"—the fascination of civilized man for his primitive, atavistic roots. What romance there is in Conrad's prose, in his celebration of such truths: "The voice of the surf heard now and then was a positive pleasure, like the speech of a brother." And in the memorable passage in which Marlow describes his excitement at setting out, at last, to meet the mysterious chief of the inner station, Kurtz:

Going up that river was like travelling back to the earliest beginnings of the world, when vegetation rioted on the earth and the big trees were kings. An empty stream, a great silence, an impenetrable forest. The air was warm, thick, heavy, sluggish. There was no joy in the brilliance of sunshine. . . . [Y]ou lost your way on that river as you would in a desert . . . till you thought yourself bewitched and cut off for ever from everything you had known once—somewhere—far away—in another existence perhaps.

The anxieties aroused by Charles Darwin's controversial, bitterly contested theory of evolution by way of natural selection, first promulgated in *Origin of Species* (1859) and subsequently in *The Descent of Man* (1871) are given tragic dramatic form in the tale of Kurtz's deterioration in the jungle, the much-acclaimed Kurtz of whom it is said by Marlow that "all of Europe had gone into [his] making." Conrad's irony is a constant throughout the narrative, like a haunting vibration beyond the sounds of words normally uttered. And what intransigent irony in Kurtz's final words, as if Shakespeare's unregenerate Edmund, or Iago, and not Lear or Othello, were the touchstones of moral truth. Dying of fever in the jungle, as Marlow nearly dies, Kurtz's famous pronouncement of his own spiritual condition—"The horror! The horror!"—is a judgment upon man's universal propensity for evil. What is this mysterious kinship that Marlow feels with the doomed man, whom he has traveled hundreds of miles to meet, only to discover him moribund, hideous? "It was as if an animated image of death carved out of old ivory had been shaking its hand with menaces at a motionless crowd of men made of dark and glittering bronze." (Compare Marlow's subterranean connection with Kurtz to the idealized and romanticized connection between the immature young captain of "The Secret Sharer" and his double, the fugitive Leggatt.) Yet, in his symbolic role as chief of the coveted inner station, Kurtz is indeed, as Marlow claims, a remarkable man:

> [H]is stare . . . was wide enough to embrace the whole universe, piercing enough to penetrate all the hearts that beat in the darkness. He had summed up—he had judged. "The horror!" . . . It was an affirmation, a moral victory paid for by innumerable defeats, by abominable terrors, by

abominable satisfactions. But it was a victory! That is why I have remained loyal to Kurtz to the last. . .

(Kurtz's real-life model was a man named Georges Antoine Klein, an employee of the Brussels-based trading company Société Anonyme Belge pour le Commerce du Haut-Congo, whom Conrad met shortly before Klein's death. His body was buried at Tchumbiri on the Congo.)

Through the prism of shimmering, musical language that is the essence of Conrad's achievement in "Heart of Darkness," the author has hoped to elevate Kurtz, a white racist murderer whose actions have parodied the idealism of his speech, to the stature of tragedy; he is one whose degradation at the end of his life can't be the sole measure of his moral worth.

Like Herman Melville, who also went to sea as a very young man, Joseph Conrad acquired in his early, impressionistic years a rich store of material to be transformed into tales and novels of exoticism, danger, and rites of passage. Born Józef Teodor Konrad Korzeniowski at Berdyczow in Podolia, Poland, on December 3, 1857, Conrad lost his parents at a young age, attended school in Cracow, and first went to sea, on a French merchant marine vessel, at the age of seventeen. He is said to have attempted suicide at the age of twenty-one, but recovered quickly and signed on with the British merchant navy for whom he would serve, at various ranks, for the next sixteen years. He became a naturalized British subject in 1886 and changed his name to Joseph Conrad; in that year he wrote his first short story, "The Black Mate." His numerous voyages took him virtually everywhere—to the West Indies, to Constantinople, to Sumatra, India, Java, Australia, Singapore; most famously, and almost fatally, to the Belgian Congo in 1890. Though desperate to earn a living, the youthful Conrad was clearly a romantic for whom sailing was an emotional, perhaps even a spiritual vocation. Surely this is Conrad speaking in the voice of Marlow, confiding in his fellow seafarers at the outset of "Heart of Darkness":

> Now when I was a little chap I had a passion for maps. I would look for hours at South America, or Africa, or Australia, and lose myself in all the glories of exploration. At that time there were many blank spaces on the earth, and when I saw one that looked particularly inviting on a map (but they all look that) I would put my finger on it and say, "When I grow up I will go there."

By the time Marlow had grown up, however, Africa had "ceased to be a blank space of delightful mystery. . . . It had become a place of darkness. But there was in it one river especially . . . resembling an immense snake uncoiled, with its head in the sea, its body at rest curving afar over a vast country, and its tail lost in the depths of the land." This great river, the Congo, fascinates Marlow "as a snake would a bird."

In June 1890, Conrad was appointed captain of a river steamer on the Congo; ominously, his predecessor had been butchered by native Africans and his body left to rot unburied in the jungle. Conrad's difficult four-mouth adventure, recorded more or less faithfully in "Heart of Darkness," left him near death, devastated with dysentery and fever; his health was broken for the remainder of his life. Conrad's predilection for extreme pessimism, depression, and anxiety would seem to have been exacerbated by his physical condition. In May 1891, for instance, following his return in Europe, he confided in a letter to a friend, "I am still plunged in deepest night, and my dreams are only nightmares." (See *Conrad* by Norman Sherry, Thames & Hudson, 1972.)

Yet the experience was transforming to Conrad, comparable to the experience of writers who have seen armed combat firsthand or have been wounded in battle, for Conrad would one day claim that "before the Congo, I was just an animal." By the end of 1894, Conrad had retired from seafaring; his first novel, *Almayer's Folly,* was published and well received in 1895. His remarkable career had begun.

Though always a controversial figure, criticized in some quarters for his intensely poetic, frequently rhetorical prose and for the unremitting pessimism of certain of his works, Conrad is generally acclaimed as one of the progenitors, along with his mentors Gustave Flaubert and Henry James, of the Modernist novel; he has been called a master of the psychological novel, the political novel, and the "intellectual mystery" novel; the fastidiously rendered prose of such works as *The Nigger of the "Narcissus,"* "Heart of Darkness" and *Nostromo,* among others, identifies him as a writer for whom language is a kind of music, rendered with a poet's ear. Following Henry James's example in his essay "The Art of Fiction" (1888), Conrad set out, in his Preface to *The Nigger of the "Narcissus"* (1897), to establish his belief in the alliance in prose fiction of the moral and the aesthetic; his elevation of the writing life is extreme, suggesting almost a religious, or mystical, vocation; the artist is one who snatches "in a moment of courage . . . a passing phase of life" in the effort of showing life's "vibration, its color, its form; and through its movement, its form, and its color, reveal[s] the substance of its truth."

By the time of Conrad's death in 1924, in Canterbury, England, this Polish-born emigrant for whom English was not his first or even his second language, would be celebrated as one of the greatest of English novelists, revered as a classic in his own time.

Since its initial publication in 1902, in the volume *Youth,* Conrad's most meticulously poetic work of fiction, "Heart of Darkness," has acquired an extraordinary reputation. Nine decades after its publication it remains one of the most read, and debated, of English works of fiction; it was the model, in spirit, of the flawed but enormously ambitious film by Francis Ford Coppola, *Apocalypse Now** (1979); it has easily become the surpassing masterwork of Conrad's distinguished career, displacing even *The Nigger of the "Narcissus," Lord Jim* (1900), *Nostromo* (1904), *The Secret Agent* (1907), *Victory* (1915), and such brilliantly realized tales as "The Secret Sharer" and "An Outpost of Progress." Part of this is due, of course, to the novella's brevity; like Henry James's *The Turn of the Screw,* it is a feat of dramatic compression in which virtually every passage, if not every sentence, moves us ineluctably toward our moment of revelation: the unmasking of Kurtz, and his twin, terrible pronouncements, "Exterminate all the brutes!" and "The horror! The horror!" (The latter has achieved a kind of transcultural autonomy, very like Edvard Munch's 1895 woodcut "The Scream"—a bleakly comic shorthand for twentieth-century angst.)

Unlike other, longer works of Conrad's that provide the reader with imbricated layers of exposition, history, psychology, and description, "Heart of Darkness" moves swiftly forward as Marlow's journey moves him, by starts and stops, forward; this is an adventure/mystery story set in the most exotic of locales and fueled by a nightmare logic. The reader is meant to replicate Marlow's voyage as he journeys up the Congo in a snakelike passage into the depths of a formerly blank, unmapped territory: the human soul.

In recent years, Joseph Conrad's work, or more specifically, ideas of gender, race, class, and hegemony implicit in his work, have been severely criticized. The assumptions of Caucasian male privilege are no longer

---

*Coppola transformed "Heart of Darkness" into a grotesque melodrama set in Vietnam in the waning years of the Vietnam War. In the role of Marlow, an American army officer is sent to Cambodia to assassinate a renegade Green Beret colonel who has set himself up, like Kurtz, as a murderous madman-god. Imaginative in concept and vivid in execution, *Apocalypse Now* is undermined by the ludicrous overacting of Marlon Brando in the role of Kurtz, which neither he nor his director seems to have understood.

taken for granted among many readers. It should be acknowledged by Conrad's admirers that the audience for whom he imagined his work was almost exclusively male, and assuredly Caucasian. To readers not in this category, the occasionally dogmatic and even derisive nature of certain of Marlow's remarks will strike a discordant note:

> It's queer how out of touch with truth women are. They live in a world of their own, and there never has been anything like it, and never can be. It is too beautiful altogether, and if they were to set it up it would go to pieces before the first sunset. Some confounded fact we men have been living contentedly with ever since the day of creation would start up and knock the whole thing over.

Leaving aside for the moment the improbability of an entire sex, and that the child-bearing sex, being permanently "out of touch with truth," we might assume, for argument's sake, that Marlow is speaking critically of a financially well-off, minimally educated class of women who, being denied the possibility of careers and any measure of autonomy apart from fathers, husbands, brothers, or sons, were kept in a perpetual state of childish dependence upon men—the "fact"-bearing sex. In the gothic-melodramatic final scene of Marlow's tale, in which he visits Kurtz's fiancée, the very emblem of Victorian moral hypocrisy and delusion, Conrad's misogyny is disguised by an air of pity and condescension; a full year after Kurtz's ignoble death, his intended is still in mourning, a neurasthenic apparition in black, with "a pale head, floating towards me in the dusk. . . . She carried her sorrowful head as if she were proud of that sorrow." The valiant Marlow, who detests lies, for lies are "tainted with death," nonetheless "laid the ghosts of [Kurtz's] gifts at last with a lie" by telling Kurtz's intended that, at the end of Kurtz's life, it was her name he uttered. (In fact, ironically, Kurtz's last words were "The horror! The horror!") Men must lie to women, Conrad argues, to preserve women's childlike state of delusion. In Conrad's ranked moral universe, men of a certain class are custodians of truth, facts, ideas, and the respect for tradition outlined in the British Navy handbook *An Inquiry into Some Points of Seamanship*; women are associated with lies, subterfuge, hypocrisy. (Caucasian women, that is. For a portrait of a black woman, consider Marlow's description of Kurtz's native mistress, of whom Marlow speaks awkwardly as "barbarous"— "savage and superb, wild-eyed and magnificent"—with a face that communicates a "tragic and fierce aspect of wild sorrow and of dumb pain mingled with the fear of some struggling, half-shaped resolve"—"like the wilderness itself, with an air of brooding over an inscrutable purpose." Words piled upon words, suggesting a generalized allegorical figure, a carved wooden sculpture symbolizing African Woman, and not a living, breathing individual woman who is supposed to be passionately in love with the dying Kurtz.)

Conrad has been criticized more sharply for his presentations of men and women of color. Consider Marlow's astonishment and amusement when a black African emulates "white" behavior:

> I had to look after the savage who was fireman. He was an improved specimen; he could fire up a vertical boiler. . . . [T]o look at him was as edifying as seeing a dog in a parody of breeches and a feather hat, walking on his hind-legs. . . . [H]e had filed teeth, too, the poor devil, and the wool of his pate shaved into queer patterns, and three ornamental scars on each of his cheeks. He ought to have been clapping his hands and stamping his feet on the bank, instead of which he was hard at work, a thrall to strange witchcraft.

Elsewhere, African natives are "dusty niggers," "surly niggers," "cannibals." Conrad, the moralist, the artist for whom prose fiction is a vocation like the priesthood, painfully reveals himself in such passages, and numerous others, as an unquestioning heir of centuries of Caucasian bigotry. Yet it might be argued that Marlow, for all his condescension, represents a degree of humanity not found in the other Caucasian Europeans who are intent upon wresting from black Africa all they can get. Marlow isn't in the Congo for ivory, or money, or to advance his career; he takes on the captaincy of the steamboat for adventure's sake, and becomes fascinated with the demonic figure of Kurtz, the very embodiment of European civilization. Marlow's sharp, cinematic eye brings alive for us these suffering black men, whose plight is meant to move the hearts of Conrad's educated, well-to-do English readers:

> Six black men advanced in a file, toiling up the path. . . . I could see every rib, the joints of their limbs were like knots in a rope; each had an iron collar on his neck, and all were connected together with a chain whose bights swung between them, rhythmically clinking. . . . [T]hese men could by no stretch of imagination be called enemies. They were called criminals. . . . They passed me within six inches, without a glance, with that complete, deathlike indifference of unhappy savages.

Other black men, enslaved and driven like animals until they are of no further use, are allowed to crawl off and die. Marlow is horrified by these "moribund shapes"—"phantoms"—dying of exhaustion and malnutrition "as in some picture of a massacre or a pestilence." Yet we wait in vain for Marlow to protest to anyone, though he soon encounters the chief accountant of the station, an impeccably dressed and groomed Englishman. There is the suggestion in "Heart of Darkness," as elsewhere in Conrad's work, of a pessimism so deeply entrenched as to be identical with a self-serving political conservatism that conveniently renders any form of activism, even protest, ineffective.

For if all men harbor darkness in their hearts, why try to save them? Why even pity them?

The famous tale "The Secret Sharer," from Conrad's collection *'Twixt Land and Sea* (1912), similarly reflects the narrowness of its creator's perspective. Here it is class, not sex or race, that determines a man's worth: an immature young captain, uneasy in his responsibility, mysteriously protects a fugitive named Leggatt, who has fled another ship after having killed a man; the young captain goes to extraordinary, foolhardy risks to allow Leggatt to escape being brought back to England to be tried; by the end of the suspense story, with the flight of Leggatt, the equation between the two men, forged out of their similar backgrounds and temperaments, has been many times reiterated: Leggatt swims clear of the ship "as though he were my second self . . . a free man, a proud swimmer striking out for a new destiny."

The difficulty for contemporary readers of "The Secret Sharer," which was one of Conrad's favorites among his own stories, is that the bond immediately forged between the young captain and the young fugitive is class-ordained and narcissistic: Leggatt has even attended the captain's school, Conway ("You're a Conway boy?"). Leggatt's act of violence is portrayed as a virtuous act by an upstanding if hot-headed first mate; the man he has killed is of a lower social rank, one of the common sailors: "He wouldn't do his duty and wouldn't let anybody else do theirs. . . . You know well the sort of ill-conditioned snarling cur—" Why does the young captain so eagerly take Leggatt at his own word, and make no attempt to verify the story?

> He appealed to me as if our experiences had been as identical as our clothes. And I knew well enough the pestiferous danger of such a character where there are no means of legal repression. And I knew well enough also that my double there was no homicidal ruffian. I did not think of asking him for details, and he told me the story roughly in brusque,

disconnected sentences. I needed no more. I saw it all going on as though I were myself inside that other sleeping suit.

Where the Doppelgänger ("double") relationship between Marlow and Kurtz is mysterious, subtle, and ever-shifting in its meanings, the relationship between the captain and Leggatt is superficial and far too heavily underscored. But "The Secret Sharer" remains one of Conrad's most characteristic stories, and it contains passages of language as beautifully evocative as the most celebrated passages in "Heart of Darkness." The opening is particularly effective, setting the tone for a tale of solitary risk and initiation:

On my right hand there were lines of fishing stakes resembling a mysterious system of half-submerged bamboo fences, incomprehensible in its division of the domain of tropical fishes, and crazy of aspect as if abandoned forever by some nomad tribe . . . for there was no sign of human habitation as far as the eye could reach.

The silent approach of Leggatt, like a phantom in a dream:

The side of the ship made an opaque belt of shadow on the darkling glassy shimmer of the sea. But I saw at once something elongated and pale floating very close to the ladder. Before I could form a guess a faint flash of phosphorescent light, which seemed to issue suddenly from the naked body of a man, flickered in the sleeping water with the elusive, silent play of summer lightning in a night sky. With a gasp I saw revealed to my stare a pair of feet, the long legs, a broad livid back immersed right up to the neck in a greenish cadaverous glow. One hand, awash, clutched the bottom rung of the ladder. He was complete except for the head. A headless corpse!

As if the young captain is the "head," the consciousness; and the romantic fugitive Leggatt the "body,"
the physical being and "secret sharer."

If Conrad's ideal in writing is to make us *see,* "The
Secret Sharer," as brilliantly as "Heart of Darkness,"
frequently fulfills that ideal.

All enduring works of art—whether Homer's *Iliad*
and *Odyssey,* the tragedies of William Shakespeare,
the popular novels of Honoré de Balzac, Charles
Dickens, Mark Twain, as well as the more literary,
esoteric novels of Joseph Conrad, Virginia Woolf, and
James Joyce—bear the imprint of their time, place,
and social perspective. All art is selective and therefore, from some perspective, unfair; no art can be universal, for no artist is universal; we are all local
individuals, shaped by the customs of our tribes. The
enduring artist is the creator not of perfect works but
of works that transcend the circumstances of their creation and contribute to the aesthetic development of
their craft. One need not identify with a writer's cul-
tural perspective to recognize that he or she may be
possessed of unique, valuable gifts; like Joseph Conrad, an artist whose fiction repays close and repeated
readings and whose unsparing tragic vision has a particular resonance for the twentieth century with its
blood-tide of history—the devastation of two world
wars and countless nearly continuous smaller wars, the
unspeakable horror of the Holocaust, the slaughter of
hundreds of millions of men, women and children in
the service of deranged totalitarian "ideals." Joseph
Conrad is one of the great visionaries bearing witness
to the predicament of civilized man: how to match the
"technique" and "method" so ironically celebrated in
"Heart of Darkness" with a corresponding humanity
that acknowledges, but does not succumb to, man's
flawed and treacherous soul.

—Joyce Carol Oates

The Secret Sharer

I

On my right hand there were lines of fishing stakes resembling a mysterious system of half-submerged bamboo fences, incomprehensible in its division of the domain of tropical fishes, and crazy of aspect as if abandoned forever by some nomad tribe of fishermen now gone to the other end of the ocean; for there was no sign of human habitation as far as the eye could reach. To the left a group of barren islets, suggesting ruins of stone walls, towers, and blockhouses, had its foundations set in a blue sea that itself looked solid, so still and stable did it lie below my feet; even the track of light from the westering sun shone smoothly, without that animated glitter which tells of an imperceptible ripple. And when I turned my head to take a parting glance at the tug which had just left us anchored outside the bar, I saw the straight line of the flat shore joined to the stable sea, edge to edge, with a perfect and unmarked closeness, in one leveled floor half brown, half blue under the enormous dome of the sky. Corresponding in their insignificance to the islets of the sea, two small clumps of trees, one on each side of the only fault in the impeccable joint, marked the mouth of the river Meinam we had just left on the first preparatory stage of our homeward journey; and, far back on the inland level, a larger and loftier mass, the grove surrounding the great Paknam pagoda, was the only thing on which the eye could rest from the vain task of exploring the monotonous

3

sweep of the horizon. Here and there gleams as of a few scattered pieces of silver marked the windings of the great river; and on the nearest of them, just within the bar, the tug steaming right into the land became lost to my sight, hull and funnel and masts, as though the impassive earth had swallowed her up without an effort, without a tremor. My eye followed the light cloud of her smoke, now here, now there, above the plain, according to the devious curves of the stream, but always fainter and farther away, till I lost it at last behind the miter-shaped hill of the great pagoda. And then I was left alone with my ship, anchored at the head of the Gulf of Siam.

She floated at the starting point of a long journey, very still in an immense stillness, the shadows of her spars flung far to the eastward by the setting sun. At that moment I was alone on her decks. There was not a sound in her—and around us nothing moved, nothing lived, not a canoe on the water, not a bird in the air, not a cloud in the sky. In this breathless pause at the threshold of a long passage we seemed to be measuring our fitness for a long and arduous enterprise, the appointed task of both our existences to be carried out, far from all human eyes, with only sky and sea for spectators and for judges.

There must have been some glare in the air to interfere with one's sight, because it was only just before the sun left us that my roaming eyes made out beyond the highest ridges of the principal islet of the group something which did away with the solemnity of perfect solitude. The tide of darkness flowed on swiftly; and with tropical suddenness a swarm of stars came out above the shadowy earth, while I lingered yet, my hand resting lightly on my ship's rail as if on the shoulder of a trusted friend. But, with all that multitude of celestial bodies staring down at one, the comfort of quiet communion with her was gone for good. And there were also disturbing sounds by this time—voices, footsteps, forward; the steward flitted along the main-deck, a busily ministering spirit; a hand bell tinkled urgently under the poop deck. . . .

I found my two officers waiting for me near the supper table, in the lighted cuddy. We sat down at once, and as I helped the chief mate, I said:

"Are you aware that there is a ship anchored inside the islands? I saw her mastheads above the ridge as the sun went down."

He raised sharply his simple face, overcharged by a terrible growth of whisker, and emitted his usual ejaculations: "Bless my soul, sir! You don't say so!"

My second mate was a round-cheeked, silent young man, grave beyond his years, I thought; but as our eyes happened to meet I detected a slight quiver on his lips. I looked down at once. It was not my part to encourage sneering on board my ship. It must be said, too, that I knew very little of my officers. In consequence of certain events of no particular significance, except to myself, I had been appointed to the command only a fortnight before. Neither did I know much of the hands forward. All these people had been together for eighteen months or so, and my position was that of the only stranger on board. I mention this because it has some bearing on what is to follow. But what I felt most was my being a stranger to the ship; and if all the truth must be told, I was somewhat of a stranger to myself. The youngest man on board (barring the second mate), and untried as yet by a position of the fullest responsibility, I was willing to take the adequacy of the others for granted. They had simply to be equal to their tasks; but I wondered how far I should turn out faithful to that ideal conception of one's own personality every man sets up for himself secretly.

Meantime the chief mate, with an almost visible effect of collaboration on the part of his round eyes and frightful whiskers, was trying to evolve a theory of the anchored ship. His dominant trait was to take all things into earnest consideration. He was of a pains-taking turn of mind. As he used to say, he "liked to account to himself" for practically everything that came in his way, down to a miserable scorpion he had found in his cabin a week before. The why and the wherefore of that scorpion—how it got on board and came to select his room rather than the pantry (which was a dark place and more what a scorpion would be partial to), and how on earth it managed to drown itself in the inkwell of his writing desk—had exercised him infinitely. The ship within the islands was much more easily accounted for; and just as we were about to rise from table he made his pronouncement. She was, he doubted not, a ship from home lately arrived. Probably she drew too much water to cross the bar except at the top of spring tides. Therefore she went into that natural harbor to wait for a few days in pref-erence to remaining in an open roadstead.

"That's so," confirmed the second mate, suddenly, in his slightly hoarse voice. "She draws over twenty feet. She's the Liverpool ship *Sephora* with a cargo of coal. Hundred and twenty-three days from Cardiff."

We looked at him in surprise.

"The tugboat skipper told me when he came on board for your letters, sir," explained the young man. "He expects to take her up the river the day after tomorrow."

After thus overwhelming us with the extent of his information he slipped out of the cabin. The mate observed regretfully that he "could not account for that young fellow's whims." What prevented him tell-ing us all about it at once, he wanted to know.

I detained him as he was making a move. For the last two days the crew had had plenty of hard work, and the night before they had very little sleep. I felt painfully that I—a stranger—was doing something un-usual when I directed him to let all hands turn in without setting an anchor watch. I proposed to keep on deck myself till one o'clock or thereabouts. I would get the second mate to relieve me at that hour.

"He will turn out the cook and the steward at four," I concluded, "and then give you a call. Of course at the slightest sign of any sort of wind we'll have the hands up and make a start at once."

He concealed his astonishment. "Very well, sir." Outside the cuddy he put his head in the second mate's door to inform him of my unheard-of caprice to take a five hours' anchor watch on myself. I heard the other raise his voice incredulously—"What? The Captain himself?" Then a few more murmurs, a door closed, then another. A few moments later I went on deck.

My strangeness, which had made me sleepless, had prompted that unconventional arrangement, as if I had expected in those solitary hours of the night to get on terms with the ship of which I knew nothing, manned by men of whom I knew very little more. Fast alongside a wharf, littered like any ship in port with a tangle of unrelated things, invaded by unrelated shore people, I had hardly seen her yet properly. Now, as she lay cleared for sea, the stretch of her main-deck seemed to me very fine under the stars. Very fine, very roomy for her size, and very inviting. I descended the poop and paced the waist, my mind picturing to myself the coming passage through the Malay Archipelago, down the Indian Ocean, and up the Atlantic. All its phases were familiar enough to me, every characteristic, all the alternatives which were likely to face me on the high seas—everything! . . . except the novel responsibility of command. But I took heart from the reasonable thought that the ship was like other ships, the men like other men, and that the sea was not likely to keep any special surprises expressly for my discomfiture.

Arrived at that comforting conclusion, I bethought myself of a cigar and went below to get it. All was still down there. Everybody at the after end of the ship was sleeping profoundly. I came out again on the quarter-deck, agreeably at ease in my sleeping suit on that warm breathless night, barefooted, a glowing cigar in my teeth, and, going forward, I was met by the profound silence of the fore end of the ship. Only as I passed the door of the forecastle I heard a deep, quiet, trustful sigh of some sleeper inside. And suddenly I rejoiced in the great security of the sea as compared with the unrest of the land, in my choice of that untempted life presenting no disquieting problems, invested with an elementary moral beauty by the absolute straightforwardness of its appeal and by the singleness of its purpose.

The riding light in the forerigging burned with a clear, untroubled, as if symbolic, flame, confident and bright in the mysterious shades of the night. Passing on my way aft along the other side of the ship, I observed that the rope side ladder, put over, no doubt, for the master of the tug when he came to fetch away our letters, had not been hauled in as it should have been. I became annoyed at this, for exactitude in some small matters is the very soul of discipline. Then I reflected that I had myself peremptorily dismissed my officers from duty, and by my own act had prevented the anchor watch being formally set and things properly attended to. I asked myself whether it was wise ever to interfere with the established routine of duties even from the kindest of motives. My action might have made me appear eccentric. Goodness only knew how that absurdly whiskered mate would "account" for my conduct, and what the whole ship thought of that informality of their new captain. I was vexed with myself.

Not from compunction certainly, but, as it were mechanically, I proceeded to get the ladder in myself. Now a side ladder of that sort is a light affair and comes in easily, yet my vigorous tug, which should have brought it flying on board, merely recoiled upon my body in a totally unexpected jerk. What the devil! . . . I was so astounded by the immovableness of that ladder that I remained stockstill, trying to account for it to myself like that imbecile mate of mine. In the end, of course, I put my head over the rail.

The side of the ship made an opaque belt of shadow on the darkling glassy shimmer of the sea. But I saw at once something elongated and pale floating very close to the ladder. Before I could form a guess a faint flash of phosphorescent light, which seemed to issue suddenly from the naked body of a man, flickered in the sleeping water with the elusive, silent play of summer lightning in a night sky. With a gasp I saw revealed to my stare a pair of feet, the long legs, a broad livid back immersed right up to the neck in a greenish cadaverous glow. One hand, awash, clutched the bottom rung of the ladder. He was complete but for the head. A headless corpse! The cigar dropped out of my gaping mouth with a tiny plop and a short hiss quite audible in the absolute stillness of all things under heaven. At that I suppose he raised up his face, a dimly pale oval in the shadow of the ship's side. But even then I could only barely make out down there the shape of his black-haired head. However, it was enough for the horrid, frost-bound sensation which had gripped me about the chest to pass off. The moment of vain exclamations was past, too. I only climbed on the spare spar and leaned over the rail as far as I could, to bring my eyes nearer to that mystery floating alongside.

As he hung by the ladder, like a resting swimmer, the sea lightning played about his limbs at every stir; and he appeared in it ghastly, silvery, fishlike. He remained as mute as a fish, too. He made no motion to get out of the water, either. It was inconceivable that he should not attempt to come on board, and strangely troubling to suspect that perhaps he did not want to. And my first words were prompted by just that troubled incertitude.

"What's the matter?" I asked in my ordinary tone, speaking down to the face upturned exactly under mine.

"Cramp," it answered, no louder. Then slightly anxious, "I say, no need to call anyone."

"I was not going to," I said.

"Are you alone on deck?"

"Yes."

I had somehow the impression that he was on the point of letting go the ladder to swim away beyond my ken—mysterious as he came. But, for the moment, this being appearing as he had risen from the bottom of the sea (it was certainly the nearest land to the ship) wanted only to know the time. I told him. And he, down there, tentatively:

"I suppose your captain's turned in?"

"I am sure he isn't," I said.

He seemed to struggle with himself, for I heard something like the low, bitter murmur of doubt. "What's the good?" His next words came out with a hesitating effort.

"Look here, my man. Could you call him out quietly?"

I thought the time had come to declare myself.

"*I* am the captain."

I heard a "By Jove!" whispered at the level of the water. The phosphorescence flashed in the swirl of the water all about his limbs, his other hand seized the ladder.

"My name's Leggatt."

The voice was calm and resolute. A good voice. The self-possession of that man had somehow induced a corresponding state in myself. It was very quietly that I remarked:

"You must be a good swimmer."

"Yes. I've been in the water practically since nine o'clock. The question for me now is whether I am to let go this ladder and go on swimming till I sink from exhaustion, or—to come on board here."

I felt this was no mere formula of desperate speech, but a real alternative in the view of a strong soul. I should have gathered from this that he was young; indeed, it is only the young who are ever confronted by such clear issues. But at the time it was pure intuition on my part. A mysterious communication was established already between us two—in the face of that silent, darkened tropical sea. I was young, too; young enough to make no comment. The man in the water began suddenly to climb up the ladder, and I hastened away from the rail to fetch some clothes.

Before entering the cabin I stood still, listening in the lobby at the foot of the stairs. A faint snore came through the closed door of the chief mate's room. The second mate's door was on the hook, but the darkness in there was absolutely soundless. He, too, was young and could sleep like a stone. Remained the steward, but he was not likely to wake up before he was called. I got a sleeping suit out of my room and, coming back on deck, saw the naked man from the sea sitting on the main hatch, glimmering white in the darkness, his elbows on his knees and his head in his hands. In a moment he had concealed his damp body in a sleeping suit of the same gray-stripe pattern as the one I was wearing and followed me like my double on the poop. Together we moved right aft, barefooted, silent.

"What is it?" I asked in a deadened voice, taking the lighted lamp out of the binnacle, and raising it to his face.

"An ugly business."

He had rather regular features; a good mouth; light eyes under somewhat heavy, dark eyebrows; a smooth, square forehead; no growth on his cheeks; a small, brown mustache, and a well-shaped, round chin. His expression was concentrated, meditative, under the inspecting light of the lamp I held up to his face; such as a man thinking hard in solitude might wear. My sleeping suit was just right for his size. A well-knit young fellow of twenty-five at most. He caught his lower lip with the edge of white, even teeth.

"Yes," I said, replacing the lamp in the binnacle. The warm, heavy tropical night closed upon his head again.

"There's a ship over there," he murmured.

"Yes, I know. The *Sephora*. Did you know of us?"

"Hadn't the slightest idea. I am the mate of her——"
He paused and corrected himself. "I should say I
was."

"Aha! Something wrong?"

"Yes. Very wrong indeed. I've killed a man."

"What do you mean? Just now?"

"No, on the passage. Weeks ago. Thirty-nine south.
When I say a man——"

"Fit of temper," I suggested, confidently.

The shadowy, dark head, like mine, seemed to nod
imperceptibly above the ghostly gray of my sleeping
suit. It was, in the night, as though I had been faced
by my own reflection in the depths of a somber and
immense mirror.

"A pretty thing to have to own up to for a Conway
boy," murmured my double, distinctly.

"You're a Conway boy?"

"I am," he said, as if startled. Then, slowly . . .
"Perhaps you too——"

It was so; but being a couple of years older I had
left before he joined. After a quick interchange of
dates a silence fell; and I thought suddenly of my absurd mate with his terrific whiskers and the "Bless my
soul—you don't say so" type of intellect. My double
gave me an inkling of his thoughts by saying: "My
father's a parson in Norfolk. Do you see me before a
judge and jury on that charge? For myself I can't see
the necessity. There are fellows that an angel from
heaven—— And I am not that. He was one of those
creatures that are just simmering all the time with a
silly sort of wickedness. Miserable devils that have no
business to live at all. He wouldn't do his duty and
wouldn't let anybody else do theirs. But what's the
good of talking! You know well enough the sort of
ill-conditioned snarling cur——"

He appealed to me as if our experiences had been
as identical as our clothes. And I knew well enough
the pestiferous danger of such a character where there
are no means of legal repression. And I knew well
enough also that my double there was no homicidal

ruffian. I did not think of asking him for details, and he told me the story roughly in brusque, disconnected sentences. I needed no more. I saw it all going on as though I were myself inside that other sleeping suit.

"It happened while we were setting a reefed foresail, at dusk. Reefed foresail! You understand the sort of weather. The only sail we had left to keep the ship running; so you may guess what it had been like for days. Anxious sort of job, that. He gave me some of his cursed insolence at the sheet. I tell you I was overdone with this terrific weather that seemed to have no end to it. Terrific, I tell you—and a deep ship. I believe the fellow himself was half crazed with funk. It was no time for gentlemanly reproof, so I turned round and felled him like an ox. He up and at me. We closed just as an awful sea made for the ship. All hands saw it coming and took to the rigging, but I had him by the throat, and went on shaking him like a rat, the men above us yelling, 'Look out! look out!' Then a crash as if the sky had fallen on my head. They say that for over ten minutes hardly anything was to be seen of the ship—just the three masts and a bit of the forecastle head and of the poop all awash driving along in a smother of foam. It was a miracle that they found us, jammed together behind the forebitts. It's clear that I meant business, because I was holding him by the throat still when they picked us up. He was black in the face. It was too much for them. It seems they rushed us aft together, gripped as we were, screaming 'Murder!' like a lot of lunatics, and broke into the cuddy. And the ship running for her life, touch and go all the time, any minute her last in a sea fit to turn your hair gray only a-looking at it. I understand that the skipper, too, started raving like the rest of them. The man had been deprived of sleep for more than a week, and to have this sprung on him at the height of a furious gale nearly drove him out of his mind. I wonder they didn't fling me overboard after getting the carcass of their precious shipmate out of my fingers. They had rather a job to separate us, I've been told. A sufficiently fierce story to make an old judge and a respectable jury sit up a bit. The first thing I heard when I came to myself was the maddening howling of that endless gale, and on that the voice of the old man. He was hanging on to my bunk, staring into my face out of the sou'wester.

" 'Mr. Leggatt, you have killed a man. You can act no longer as chief mate of this ship.' "

His care to subdue his voice made it sound monotonous. He rested a hand on the end of the skylight to steady himself with, and all that time did not stir a limb, so far as I could see. "Nice little tale for a quiet tea party," he concluded in the same tone.

One of my hands, too, rested on the end of the skylight; neither did I stir a limb, so far as I knew. We stood less than a foot from each other. It occurred to me that if old "Bless my soul—you don't say so" were to put his head up the companion and catch sight of us, he would think he was seeing double, or imagine himself come upon a scene of weird witchcraft; the strange captain having a quiet confabulation by the wheel with his own gray ghost. I became very much concerned to prevent anything of the sort. I heard the other's soothing undertone.

"My father's a parson in Norfolk," it said. Evidently he had forgotten he had told me this important fact before. Truly a nice little tale.

"You had better slip down into my stateroom now," I said, moving off stealthily. My double followed my movements; our bare feet made no sound; I let him in, closed the door with care, and, after giving a call to the second mate, returned on deck for my relief.

"Not much sign of any wind yet," I remarked when he approached.

"No, sir. Not much," he assented, sleepily, in his hoarse voice, with just enough deference, no more, and barely suppressing a yawn.

"Well, that's all you have a look out for. You have got your orders."

"Yes, sir."

I paced a turn or two on the poop and saw him take up his position face forward with his elbow in the ratlines of the mizzen rigging before I went below. The mate's faint snoring was still going on peacefully. The cuddy lamp was burning over the table on which stood a vase with flowers, a polite attention from the ship's provision merchant—the last flowers we should see for the next three months at the very least. Two bunches of bananas hung from the beam symmetrically, one on each side of the rudder casing. Everything was as before in the ship—except that two of her captain's sleeping suits were simultaneously in use, one motionless in the cuddy, the other keeping very still in the captain's stateroom.

It must be explained here that my cabin had the form of the capital letter L, the door being within the angle and opening into the short part of the letter. A couch was to the left, the bed place to the right; my writing desk and the chronometers' table faced the door. But anyone opening it, unless he stepped right inside, had no view of what I call the long (or vertical) part of the letter. It contained some lockers surmounted by a bookcase; and a few clothes, a thick jacket or two, caps, oilskin coat, and such like, hung on hooks. There was at the bottom of that part of a door opening into my bathroom, which could be entered also directly from the saloon. But that way was never used.

The mysterious arrival had discovered the advantage of this particular shape. Entering my room, lighted strongly by a big bulkhead lamp swung on gimbals above my writing desk, I did not see him anywhere till he stepped out quietly from behind the coats hung in the recessed part.

"I heard somebody moving about, and went in there at once," he whispered.

I, too, spoke under my breath.

"Nobody is likely to come in here without knocking and getting permission."

He nodded. His face was thin and the sunburn faded,

as though he had been ill. And no wonder. He had been, I heard presently, kept under arrest in his cabin for nearly seven weeks. But there was nothing sickly in his eyes or in his expression. He was not a bit like me, really; yet, as we stood leaning over my bed place, whispering side by side, with our dark heads together and our backs to the door, anybody bold enough to open it stealthily would have been treated to the uncanny sight of a double captain busy talking in whispers with his other self.

"But all this doesn't tell me how you came to hang on to our side ladder," I inquired, in the hardly audible murmurs we used, after he had told me something more of the proceedings on board the *Sephora* once the bad weather was over.

"When we sighted Java Head I had had time to think all those matters out several times over. I had six weeks of doing nothing else, and with only an hour or so every evening for a tramp on the quarter-deck."

He whispered, his arms folded on the side of my bed place, staring through the open port. And I could imagine perfectly the manner of this thinking out—a stubborn if not a steadfast operation; something of which I should have been perfectly incapable.

"I reckoned it would be dark before we closed with the land," he continued, so low that I had to strain my hearing near as we were to each other, shoulder touching shoulder almost. "So I asked to speak to the old man. He always seemed very sick when he came to see me—as if he could not look me in the face. You know, that foresail saved the ship. She was too deep to have run long under bare poles. And it was I that managed to set it for him. Anyway, he came. When I had him in my cabin—he stood by the door looking at me as if I had the halter round my neck already—I asked him right away to leave my cabin door unlocked at night while the ship was going through Sunda Straits. There would be the Java coast within two or three miles, off Angier Point. I wanted nothing more. I've had a prize for swimming my second year in the Conway."

"I can believe it," I breathed out.

"God only knows why they locked me in every night. To see some of their faces you'd have thought they were afraid I'd go about at night strangling people. Am I a murdering brute? Do I look it? By Jove! If I had been he wouldn't have trusted himself like that into my room. You'll say I might have chucked him aside and bolted out, there and then—it was dark already. Well, no. And for the same reason I wouldn't think of trying to smash the door. There would have been a rush to stop me at the noise, and I did not mean to get into a confounded scrimmage. Somebody else might have got killed—for I would not have broken out only to get chucked back, and I did not want any more of that work. He refused, looking more sick than ever. He was afraid of the men, and also of that old second mate of his who had been sailing with him for years—a gray-headed old humbug; and his steward, too, had been with him devil knows how long—seventeen years or more—a dogmatic sort of loafer who hated me like poison, just because I was the chief mate. No chief mate ever made more than one voyage in the *Sephora,* you know. Those two old chaps ran the ship. Devil only knows what the skipper wasn't afraid of (all his nerve went to pieces altogether in that hellish spell of bad weather we had)—of what the law would do to him—of his wife, perhaps. Oh, yes! she's on board. Though I don't think she would have meddled. She would have been only too glad to have me out of the ship in any way. The 'brand of Cain' business, don't you see. That's all right. I was ready enough to go off wandering on the face of the earth—and that was price enough to pay for an Abel of that sort. Anyhow, he wouldn't listen to me. 'This thing must take its course. I represent the law here.' He was shaking like a leaf. 'So you won't?' 'No!' 'Then I hope you will be able to sleep on that,' I said, and turned my back on him. 'I wonder that *you* can,' cries he, and locks the door.

"Well after that, I couldn't. Not very well. That was three weeks ago. We have had a slow passage through the Java Sea; drifted about Carimata for ten days. When we anchored here they thought, I suppose, it was all right. The nearest land (and that's five miles) is the ship's destination; the consul would soon set about catching me; and there would have been no object in bolting to these islets there. I don't suppose there's a drop of water on them. I don't know how it was, but tonight that steward, after bringing me my supper, went out to let me eat it, and left the door unlocked. And I ate it—all there was, too. After I had finished I strolled out on the quarter-deck. I don't know that I meant to do anything. A breath of fresh air was all I wanted, I believe. Then a sudden temptation came over me. I kicked off my slippers and was in the water before I had made up my mind fairly. Somebody heard the splash and they raised an awful hullabaloo. 'He's gone! Lower the boats! He's committed suicide! No, he's swimming.' Certainly I was swimming. It's not so easy for a swimmer like me to commit suicide by drowning. I landed on the nearest islet before the boat left the ship's side. I heard them pulling about in the dark, hailing, and so on, but after a bit they gave up. Everything quieted down and the anchorage became as still as death. I sat down on a stone and began to think. I felt certain they would start searching for me at daylight. There was no place to hide on those stony things—and if there had been, what would have been the good? But now I was clear of that ship, I was not going back. So after a while I took off all my clothes, tied them up in a bundle with a stone inside, and dropped them in the deep water on the outer side of that islet. That was suicide enough for me. Let them think what they liked, but I didn't mean to drown myself. I meant to swim till I sank— but that's not the same thing. I struck out for another of these little islands, and it was from that one that I first saw your riding light. Something to swim for. I went on easily, and on the way I came upon a flat rock or two above water. In the daytime, I dare say, you might make it out with a glass from your poop. I scrambled up on it and rested myself for a bit. Then I made another start. That last spell must have been over a mile."

His whisper was getting fainter and fainter, and all the time he stared straight out through the porthole, in which there was not even a star to be seen. I had not interrupted him. There was something that made comment impossible in his narrative, or perhaps in himself; a sort of feeling, a quality, which I can't find a name for. And when he ceased, all I found was a futile whisper: "So you swam for our light?"

"Yes—straight for it. It was something to swim for. I couldn't see any stars low down because the coast was in the way, and I couldn't see the land, either. The water was like glass. One might have been swimming in a confounded thousand-feet deep cistern with no place for scrambling out anywhere; but what I didn't like was the notion of swimming round and round like a crazed bullock before I gave out; and as I didn't mean to go back . . . No. Do you see me being hauled back, stark naked, off one of these little islands by the scruff of the neck and fighting like a wild beast? Somebody would have got killed for certain, and I did not want any of that. So I went on. Then your ladder——"

"Why didn't you hail the ship?" I asked, a little louder.

He touched my shoulder lightly. Lazy footsteps came right over our heads and stopped. The second mate had crossed from the other side of the poop and might have been hanging over the rail for all we knew.

"He couldn't hear us talking—could he?" My double breathed into my very ear, anxiously.

His anxiety was an answer, a sufficient answer, to the question I had put to him. An answer containing all the difficulty of that situation. I closed the porthole

quietly, to make sure. A louder word might have been
overheard.

"Who's that?" he whispered then.

"My second mate. But I don't know much more of
the fellow than you do."

And I told him a little about myself. I had been
appointed to take charge while I least expected anything of the sort, not quite a fortnight ago. I didn't
know either the ship or the people. Hadn't had the
time in port to look about me or size anybody up.
And as to the crew, all they knew was that I was
appointed to take the ship home. For the rest, I was
almost as much of a stranger on board as himself, I
said. And at the moment I felt it most acutely. I felt
that it would take very little to make me a suspect
person in the eyes of the ship's company.

He had turned about meantime; and we, the two
strangers in the ship, faced each other in identical
attitudes.

"Your ladder——" he murmured, after a silence.
"Who'd have thought of finding a ladder hanging over
at night in a ship anchored out here! I felt just then
a very unpleasant faintness. After the life I've been
leading for nine weeks, anybody would have got out
of condition. I wasn't capable of swimming round as
far as your rudder chains. And, lo and behold! there
was a ladder to get hold of. After I gripped it I said
to myself, 'What's the good?' When I saw a man's
head looking over I thought I would swim away presently and leave him shouting—in whatever language
it was. I didn't mind being looked at. I—I liked it.
And then you speaking to me so quietly—as if you
had expected me—made me hold on a little longer. It
had been a confounded lonely time—I don't mean
while swimming. I was glad to talk a little to somebody
that didn't belong to the *Sephora*. As to asking for
the captain, that was a mere impulse. It could have
been no use, with all the ship knowing about me and
the other people pretty certain to be round here in
the morning. I don't know—I wanted to be seen, to

talk with somebody, before I went on. I don't know what I would have said. . . . 'Fine night, isn't it?' or something of the sort."

"Do you think they will be round here presently?" I asked with some incredulity.

"Quite likely," he said, faintly.

He looked extremely haggard all of a sudden. His head rolled on his shoulders.

"H'm. We shall see then. Meantime get into that bed," I whispered. "Want help? There."

It was a rather high bed place with a set of drawers underneath. This amazing swimmer really needed the lift I gave him by seizing his leg. He tumbled in, rolled over on his back, and flung one arm across his eyes. And then, with his face nearly hidden, he must have looked exactly as I used to look in that bed. I gazed upon my other self for a while before drawing across carefully the two green serge curtains which ran on a brass rod. I thought for a moment of pinning them together for greater safety, but I sat down on the couch, and once there I felt unwilling to rise and hunt for a pin. I would do it in a moment. I was extremely tired, in a peculiarly intimate way, by the strain of stealthiness, by the effort of whispering and the general secrecy of this excitement. It was three o'clock by now and I had been on my feet since nine, but I was not sleepy; I could not have gone to sleep. I sat there, fagged out, looking at the curtains, trying to clear my mind of the confused sensation of being in two places at once, and greatly bothered by an exasperating knocking in my head. It was a relief to discover suddenly that it was not in my head at all, but on the outside of the door. Before I could collect myself the words "Come in" were out of my mouth, and the steward entered with a tray, bringing in my morning coffee. I had slept, after all, and I was so frightened that I shouted, "This way! I am here, steward," as though he had been miles away. He put down the tray on the table next the couch and only then said, very quietly, "I can see you are here, sir." I felt him give me a keen look, but I dared not meet his eyes just then. He must have wondered why I had drawn the curtains of my bed before going to sleep on the couch. He went out, hooking the door open as usual.

I heard the crew washing decks above me. I knew I would have been told at once if there had been any wind. Calm, I thought, and I was doubly vexed. Indeed, I felt dual more than ever. The steward reappeared suddenly in the doorway. I jumped up from the couch so quickly that he gave a start.

"What do you want here?"

"Close your port, sir—they are washing decks."

"It is closed," I said, reddening.

"Very well, sir." But he did not move from the doorway and returned my stare in an extraordinary, equivocal manner for a time. Then his eyes wavered, all his expression changed, and in a voice unusually gentle, almost coaxingly:

"May I come in to take the empty cup away, sir?"

"Of course!" I turned my back on him while he popped in and out. Then I unhooked and closed the door and even pushed the bolt. This sort of thing could not go on very long. The cabin was as hot as an oven, too. I took a peep at my double, and discovered that he had not moved, his arm was still over his eyes; but his chest heaved; his hair was wet; his chin glistened with perspiration. I reached over him and opened the port.

"I must show myself on deck," I reflected.

Of course, theoretically, I could do what I liked, with no one to say nay to me within the whole circle of the horizon; but to lock my cabin door and take the key away I did not dare. Directly I put my head out of the companion I saw the group of my two officers, the second mate barefooted, the chief mate in long India-rubber boots, near the break of the poop, and the steward halfway down the poop ladder talking to them eagerly. He happened to catch sight of me and dived, the second ran down on the main-deck shouting some order or other, and the chief mate came to meet me, touching his cap.

There was a sort of curiosity in his eye that I did not like. I don't know whether the steward had told them that I was "queer" only, or downright drunk, but I know the man meant to have a good look at me. I watched him coming with a smile which, as he got into point-blank range, took effect and froze his very whiskers. I did not give him time to open his lips.

"Square the yards by lifts and braces before the hands go to breakfast."

It was the first particular order I had given on board that ship; and I stayed on deck to see it executed, too. I had felt the need of asserting myself without loss of time. That sneering young cub got taken down a peg or two on that occasion, and I also seized the opportunity of having a good look at the face of every foremast man as they filed past me to go to the after braces. At breakfast time, eating nothing myself, I presided with such frigid dignity that the two mates were only too glad to escape from the cabin as soon as decency permitted; and all the time the dual working of my mind distracted me almost to the point of insanity. I was constantly watching myself, my secret self, as dependent on my actions as my own personality, sleeping in that bed, behind that door which faced me as I sat at the head of the table. It was very much like being mad, only it was worse because one was aware of it.

I had to shake him for a solid minute, but when at last he opened his eyes it was in the full possession of his senses, with an inquiring look.

"All's well so far," I whispered. "Now you must vanish into the bathroom."

He did so, as noiseless as a ghost, and then I rang for the steward, and facing him boldly, directed him to tidy up my stateroom while I was having my bath— "and be quick about it." As my tone admitted of no excuses, he said, "Yes, sir," and ran off to fetch his dustpan and brushes. I took a bath and did most of my dressing, splashing, and whistling softly for the steward's edification, while the secret sharer of my life stood drawn up bolt upright in that little space, his face looking very sunken in daylight, his eyelids lowered under the stern, dark line of his eyebrows drawn together by a slight frown.

When I left him there to go back to my room the steward was finishing dusting. I sent for the mate and engaged him in some insignificant conversation. It was, as it were, trifling with the terrific character of his whiskers; but my object was to give him an opportunity for a good look at my cabin. And then I could at last shut, with a clear conscience, the door of my stateroom and get my double back into the recessed part. There was nothing else for it. He had to sit still on a small folding stool, half smothered by the heavy coats hanging there. We listened to the steward going into the bathroom out of the saloon, filling the water bottles there, scrubbing the bath, setting things to rights, whisk, bang, clatter—out again into the saloon—turn the key—click. Such was my scheme for keeping my second self invisible. Nothing better could be contrived under the circumstances. And there we sat; I at my writing desk ready to appear busy with some papers, he behind me out of sight of the door. It would not have been prudent to talk in daytime; and I could not have stood the excitement of that queer sense of whispering to myself. Now and then, glancing over my shoulder, I saw him far back there, sitting rigidly on the low stool, his bare feet close together, his arms folded, his head hanging on his breast—and perfectly still. Anybody would have taken him for me.

I was fascinated by it myself. Every moment I had to glance over my shoulder. I was looking at him when a voice outside the door said:

"Beg pardon, sir."

"Well!" . . . I kept my eyes on him, and so when the voice outside the door announced, "There's a ship's boat coming our way, sir," I saw him give a start—the first movement he had made for hours. But he did not raise his bowed head.

"All right. Get the ladder over."

I hesitated. Should I whisper something to him? But what? His immobility seemed to have been never disturbed. What could I tell him he did not know already? . . . Finally I went on deck.

II

The skipper of the *Sephora* had a thin red whisker all round his face, and the sort of complexion that goes with hair of that color; also the particular, rather smeary shade of blue in the eyes. He was not exactly a showy figure; his shoulders were high, his stature but middling—one leg slightly more bandy than the other. He shook hands, looking vaguely around. A spiritless tenacity was his main characteristic, I judged. I behaved with a politeness which seemed to disconcert him. Perhaps he was shy. He mumbled to me as if he were ashamed of what he was saying; gave his name (it was something like Archbold—but at this distance of years I hardly am sure), his ship's name, and a few other particulars of that sort, in the manner of a criminal making a reluctant and doleful confession. He had had terrible weather on the passage out—terrible—terrible—wife aboard, too.

By this time we were seated in the cabin and the steward brought in a tray with a bottle and glasses. "Thanks! No." Never took liquor. Would have some water, though. He drank two tumblerfuls. Terrible thirsty work. Ever since daylight had been exploring the islands round his ship.

"What was that for—fun?" I asked, with an appearance of polite interest.

"No!" He sighed. "Painful duty."

As he persisted in his mumbling and I wanted my

double to hear every word, I hit upon the notion of informing him that I regretted to say I was hard of hearing.

"Such a young man, too!" he nodded, keeping his smeary blue, unintelligent eyes fastened upon me. "What was the cause of it—some disease?" he inquired, without the least sympathy and as if he thought that, if so, I'd got no more than I deserved.

"Yes; disease," I admitted in a cheerful tone which seemed to shock him. But my point was gained, because he had to raise his voice to give me his tale. It is not worth while to record that version. It was just over two months since all this had happened, and he had thought so much about it that he seemed completely muddled as to its bearings, but still immensely impressed.

"What would you think of such a thing happening on board your own ship? I've had the *Sephora* for these fifteen years. I am a well-known shipmaster."

He was densely distressed—and perhaps I should have sympathized with him if I had been able to detach my mental vision from the unsuspected sharer of my cabin as though he were my second self. There he was on the other side of the bulkhead, four or five feet from us, no more, as we sat in the saloon. I looked politely at Captain Archbold (if that was his name), but it was the other I saw, in a gray sleeping suit, seated on a low stool, his bare feet close together, his arms folded, and every word said between us falling into the ears of his dark head bowed on his chest.

"I have been at sea now, man and boy, for seven-and-thirty years, and I've never heard of such a thing happening in an English ship. And that it should be my ship. Wife on board, too."

I was hardly listening to him.

"Don't you think," I said, "that the heavy sea which, you told me, came aboard just then might have killed the man? I have seen the sheer weight of a sea kill a man very neatly, by simply breaking his neck."

"Good God!" he uttered, impressively, fixing his

smeary blue eyes on me. "The sea! No man killed by the sea ever looked like that." He seemed positively scandalized at my suggestion. And as I gazed at him certainly not prepared for anything original on his part, he advanced his head close to me and thrust his tongue out at me so suddenly that I couldn't help starting back.

After scoring over my calmness in this graphic way he nodded wisely. If I had seen the sight, he assured me, I would never forget it as long as I lived. The weather was too bad to give the corpse a proper sea burial. So next day at dawn they took it up on the poop, covering its face with a bit of bunting; he read a short prayer, and then, just as it was, in its oilskins and long boots, they launched it amongst those mountainous seas that seemed ready every moment to swallow up the ship herself and the terrified lives on board of her.

"That reefed foresail saved you," I threw in.

"Under God—it did," he exclaimed fervently. "It was by a special mercy, I firmly believe, that it stood some of those hurricane squalls."

"It was the setting of that sail which——" I began.

"God's own hand in it," he interrupted me. "Nothing less could have done it. I don't mind telling you that I hardly dared give the order. It seemed impossible that we could touch anything without losing it, and then our last hope would have been gone."

The terror of that gale was on him yet. I let him go on for a bit, then said, casually—as if returning to a minor subject:

"You were very anxious to give up your mate to the shore people, I believe?"

He was. To the law. His obscure tenacity on that point had in it something incomprehensible and a little awful; something, as it were, mystical, quite apart from his anxiety that he should not be suspected of "countenancing any doings of that sort." Seven-and-thirty virtuous years at sea, of which over twenty of immaculate command, and the last fifteen in the *Sephora*, seemed to have laid him under some pitiless obligation.

"And you know," he went on, groping shamefacedly amongst his feelings, "I did not engage that young fellow. His people had some interest with my owners. I was in a way forced to take him on. He looked very smart, very gentlemanly, and all that. But do you know—I never liked him, somehow. I am a plain man. You see, he wasn't exactly the sort for the chief mate of a ship like the *Sephora.*"

I had become so connected in thoughts and impressions with the secret sharer of my cabin that I felt as if I, personally, were being given to understand that I, too, was not the sort that would have done for the chief mate of a ship like the *Sephora.* I had no doubt of it in my mind.

"Not at all the style of man. You understand," he insisted, superfluously, looking hard at me.

I smiled urbanely. He seemed at a loss for a while.

"I suppose I must report a suicide."

"Beg pardon?"

"Sui-cide! That's what I'll have to write to my owners directly I get in."

"Unless you manage to recover him before tomorrow," I assented, dispassionately. . . . "I mean, alive."

He mumbled something which I really did not catch, and I turned my ear to him in a puzzled manner. He fairly bawled:

"The land—I say, the mainland is at least seven miles off my anchorage."

"About that."

My lack of excitement, of curiosity, of surprise, of any sort of pronounced interest, began to arouse his distrust. But except for the felicitous pretense of deafness I had not tried to pretend anything. I had felt utterly incapable of playing the part of ignorance properly, and therefore was afraid to try. It is also certain that he had brought some ready-made suspicions with him, and that he viewed my politeness as a strange and unnatural phenomenon. And yet how

else could I have received him? Not heartily! That was
impossible for psychological reasons, which I need not
state here. My only object was to keep off his inquiries. Surlily? Yes, but surliness might have provoked a
point-blank question. From its novelty to him and
from its nature, punctilious courtesy was the manner
best calculated to restrain the man. But there was the
danger of his breaking through my defense bluntly. I
could not, I think, have met him by a direct lie, also
for psychological (not moral) reasons. If he had only
known how afraid I was of his putting my feeling of
identity with the other to the test! But, strangely
enough—(I thought of it only afterwards)—I believe
that he was not a little disconcerted by the reverse
side of that weird situation, by something in me that
reminded him of the man he was seeking—suggested
a mysterious similitude to the young fellow he had
distrusted and disliked from the first.

However that might have been, the silence was not
very prolonged. He took another oblique step.

"I reckon I had no more than a two-mile pull to
your ship. Not a bit more."

"And quite enough, too, in this awful heat," I said.

Another pause full of mistrust followed. Necessity,
they say, is mother of invention, but fear, too, is not
barren of ingenious suggestions. And I was afraid he
would ask me point-blank for news of my other self.

"Nice little saloon, isn't it?" I remarked, as if noticing for the first time the way his eyes roamed from
one closed door to the other. "And very well fitted
out, too. Here, for instance," I continued, reaching
over the back of my seat negligently and flinging the
door open, "is my bathroom."

He made an eager movement, but hardly gave it a
glance. I got up, shut the door of the bathroom, and
invited him to have a look round, as if I were very
proud of my accommodation. He had to rise and be
shown round, but he went through the business without any raptures whatever.

"And now we'll have a look at my stateroom," I

declared, in a voice as loud as I dared to make it, crossing the cabin to the starboard side with purposely heavy steps.

He followed me in and gazed around. My intelligent double had vanished. I played my part.

"Very convenient—isn't it?"

"Very nice. Very comf . . ." He didn't finish and went out brusquely as if to escape from some unrighteous wiles of mine. But it was not to be. I had been too frightened not to feel vengeful; I felt I had him on the run, and I meant to keep him on the run. My polite insistence must have had something menacing in it, because he gave in suddenly. And I did not let him off a single item; mate's room, pantry, storerooms, the very sail locker which was also under the poop— he had to look into them all. When at last I showed him out on the quarter-deck he drew a long, spiritless sigh, and mumbled dismally that he must really be going back to his ship now. I desired my mate, who had joined us, to see to the captain's boat.

The man of whiskers gave a blast on the whistle which he used to wear hanging round his neck, and yelled, "*Sephora*'s away!" My double down there in my cabin must have heard, and certainly could not feel more relieved than I. Four fellows came running out from somewhere forward and went over the side, while my own men, appearing on deck too, lined the rail. I escorted my visitor to the gangway ceremoniously, and nearly overdid it. He was a tenacious beast. On the very ladder he lingered, and in that unique, guiltily conscientious manner of sticking to the point:

"I say . . . you . . . you don't think that——"

I covered his voice loudly:

"Certainly not. . . . I am delighted. Good-by."

I had an idea of what he meant to say, and just saved myself by the privilege of defective hearing. He was too shaken generally to insist, but my mate, close witness of that parting, looked mystified and his face took on a thoughtful cast. As I did not want to appear as if I wished to avoid all communication with my officers, he had the opportunity to address me.

"Seems a very nice man. His boat's crew told our chaps a very extraordinary story, if what I am told by the steward is true. I suppose you had it from the captain, sir?"

"Yes. I had a story from the captain."

"A very horrible affair—isn't it, sir?"

"It is."

"Beats all these tales we hear about murders in Yankee ships."

"I don't think it beats them. I don't think it resembles them in the least."

"Bless my soul—you don't say so! But of course I've no acquaintance whatever with American ships, not I, so I couldn't go against your knowledge. It's horrible enough for me. . . . But the queerest part is that those fellows seemed to have some idea the man was hidden aboard here. They had really. Did you ever hear of such a thing?"

"Preposterous—isn't it?"

We were walking to and fro athwart the quarter-deck. No one of the crew forward could be seen (the day was Sunday), and the mate pursued:

"There was some little dispute about it. Our chaps took offense. 'As if we would harbor a thing like that,' they said. 'Wouldn't you like to look for him in our coal-hole?' Quite a tiff. But they made it up in the end. I suppose he did drown himself. Don't you, sir?"

"I don't suppose anything."

"You have no doubt in the matter, sir?"

"None whatever."

I left him suddenly. I felt I was producing a bad impression, but with my double down there it was most trying to be on deck. And it was almost as trying to be below. Altogether a nerve-trying situation. But on the whole I felt less torn in two when I was with him. There was no one in the whole ship whom I dared take into my confidence. Since the hands had

got to know his story, it would have been impossible
to pass him off for anyone else, and an accidental
discovery was to be dreaded now more than ever. . . .

The steward being engaged in laying the table for
dinner, we could talk only with our eyes when I first
went down. Later in the afternoon we had a cautious
try at whispering. The Sunday quietness of the ship
was against us; the stillness of air and water around
her was against us; the elements, the men were against
us—everything was against us in our secret partnership; time itself—for this could not go on forever. The
very trust in Providence was, I suppose, denied to his
guilt. Shall I confess that this thought cast me down
very much? And as to the chapter of accidents which
counts for so much in the book of success, I could
only hope that it was closed. For what favorable accident could be expected?

"Did you hear everything?" were my first words as
soon as we took up our position side by side, leaning
over my bed place.

He had. And the proof of it was his earnest whisper,
"The man told you he hardly dared to give the order."

I understood the reference to be to that saving
foresail.

"Yes. He was afraid of it being lost in the setting."

"I assure you he never gave the order. He may
think he did, but he never gave it. He stood there
with me on the break of the poop after the main top-
sail blew away, and whimpered about our last hope—
positively whimpered about it and nothing else—and
the night coming on! To hear one's skipper go on like
that in such weather was enough to drive any fellow
out of his mind. It worked me up into a sort of desperation. I just took it into my own hands and went away
from him, boiling, and—— But what's the use telling
you? *You* know! . . . Do you think that if I had not
been pretty fierce with them I should have got the
men to do anything? Not I! The bo's'n perhaps? Perhaps! It wasn't a heavy sea—it was a sea gone mad!
I suppose the end of the world will be something like

that; and a man may have the heart to see it coming once and be done with it—but to have to face it day after day—— I don't blame anybody. I was precious little better than the rest. Only—I was an officer of that old coal wagon, anyhow——"

"I quite understand," I conveyed that sincere assurance into his ear. He was out of breath with whispering; I could hear him pant slightly. It was all very simple. The same strung-up force which had given twenty-four men a chance, at least, for their lives, had, in a sort of recoil, crushed an unworthy mutinous existence.

But I had no leisure to weigh the merits of the matter—footsteps in the saloon, a heavy knock. "There's enough wind to get under way with, sir." Here was the call of a new claim upon my thoughts and even upon my feelings.

"Turn the hands up," I cried through the door. "I'll be on deck directly."

I was going out to make the acquaintance of my ship. Before I left the cabin our eyes met—the eyes of the only two strangers on board. I pointed to the recessed part where the little campstool awaited him and laid my finger on my lips. He made a gesture—somewhat vague—a little mysterious, accompanied by a faint smile, as if of regret.

This is not the place to enlarge upon the sensations of a man who feels for the first time a ship move under his feet to his own independent word. In my case they were not unalloyed. I was not wholly alone with my command; for there was that stranger in my cabin. Or rather, I was not completely and wholly with her. Part of me was absent. That mental feeling of being in two places at once affected me physically as if the mood of secrecy had penetrated my very soul. Before an hour had elapsed since the ship had begun to move, having occasion to ask the mate (he stood by my side) to take a compass bearing of the pagoda, I caught myself reaching up to his ears in whispers. I say I caught myself, but enough had escaped to startle the man. I can't describe it otherwise than by saying that he shied. A grave, preoccupied manner, as though he were in possession of some perplexing intelligence, did not leave him henceforth. A little later I moved away from the rail to look at the compass with such a stealthy gait that the helmsman noticed it—and I could not help noticing the unusual roundness of his eyes. These are trifling instances, though it's to no commander's advantage to be suspected of ludicrous eccentricities. But I was also more seriously affected. There are to a seaman certain words, gestures, that should in given conditions come as naturally, as instinctively as the winking of a menaced eye. A certain order should spring on to his lips without thinking; a certain sign should get itself made, so to speak, without reflection. But all unconscious alertness had abandoned me. I had to make an effort of will to recall myself back (from the cabin) to the conditions of the moment. I felt that I was appearing an irresolute commander to those people who were watching me more or less critically.

And, besides, there were the scares. On the second day out, for instance, coming off the deck in the afternoon (I had straw slippers on my bare feet) I stopped at the open pantry door and spoke to the steward. He was doing something there with his back to me. At the sound of my voice he nearly jumped out of his skin, as the saying is, and incidentally broke a cup.

"What on earth's the matter with you?" I asked, astonished.

He was extremely confused. "Beg your pardon, sir. I made sure you were in your cabin."

"You see I wasn't."

"No, sir. I could have sworn I had heard you moving in there not a moment ago. It's most extraordinary . . . very sorry, sir."

I passed on with an inward shudder. I was so identified with my secret double that I did not even mention the fact in those scanty, fearful whispers we exchanged. I suppose he had made some slight noise of some kind or other. It would have been miraculous if he hadn't at one time or another. And yet, haggard as he appeared, he looked always perfectly self-controlled, more than calm—almost invulnerable. On my suggestion he remained almost entirely in the bathroom, which, upon the whole, was the safest place. There could be really no shadow of an excuse for anyone ever wanting to go in there, once the steward had done with it. It was a very tiny place. Sometimes he reclined on the floor, his legs bent, his head sustained on one elbow. At others I would find him on the campstool, sitting in his gray sleeping suit and with his cropped dark hair like a patient, unmoved convict. At night I would smuggle him into my bed place, and we would whisper together, with the regular footfalls of the officer of the watch passing and repassing over our heads. It was an infinitely miserable time. It was lucky that some tins of fine preserves were stowed in a locker in my stateroom; hard bread I could always get hold of; and so he lived on stewed chicken, *pâté de foie gras,* asparagus, cooked oysters, sardines— on all sorts of abominable sham delicacies out of tins. My early-morning coffee he always drank; and it was all I dared do for him in that respect.

Every day there was the horrible maneuvering to go through so that my room and then the bathroom should be done in the usual way. I came to hate the sight of the steward, to abhor the voice of that harmless man. I felt that it was he who would bring on the disaster of discovery. It hung like a sword over our heads.

The fourth day out, I think (we were then working down the east side of the Gulf of Siam, tack for tack, in light winds and smooth water)—the fourth day, I say, of this miserable juggling with the unavoidable, as we sat at our evening meal, that man, whose slightest movement I dreaded, after putting down the dishes ran up on deck busily. This could not be dangerous. Presently he came down again; and then it appeared that he had remembered a coat of mine which I had thrown over a rail to dry after having been wetted in a shower which had passed over the ship in the afternoon. Sitting stolidly at the head of the table I became terrified at the sight of the garment on his arm. Of course he made for my door. There was no time to lose.

"Steward," I thundered. My nerves were so shaken that I could not govern my voice and conceal my agitation. This was the sort of thing that made my terrifically whiskered mate tap his forehead with his forefinger. I had detected him using that gesture while talking on deck with a confidential air to the carpenter. It was too far to hear a word, but I had no doubt that this pantomime could only refer to the strange new captain.

"Yes, sir." The pale-faced steward turned resignedly to me. It was this maddening course of being shouted at, checked without rhyme or reason, arbitrarily chased out of my cabin, suddenly called into it, sent flying out of his pantry on incomprehensible errands, that accounted for the growing wretchedness of his expression.

"Where are you going with that coat?"

"To your room, sir."

"Is there another shower coming?"

"I'm sure I don't know, sir. Shall I go up again and see, sir?"

"No! never mind."

My object was attained, as of course my other self in there would have heard everything that passed. During this interlude my two officers never raised their eyes off their respective plates; but the lip of that confounded cub, the second mate, quivered visibly.

I expected the steward to hook my coat on and come out at once. He was very slow about it; but I dominated my nervousness sufficiently not to shout after him. Suddenly I became aware (it could be heard plainly enough) that the fellow for some reason or other was opening the door of the bathroom. It was the end. The place was literally not big enough to swing a cat in. My voice died in my throat and I went

stony all over. I expected to hear a yell of surprise
and terror, and made a movement, but had not the
strength to get on my legs. Everything remained still.
Had my second self taken the poor wretch by the
throat? I don't know what I would have done next
moment if I had not seen the steward come out of
my room, close the door, and then stand quietly by
the sideboard.

"Saved," I thought. "But, no! Lost! Gone! He was
gone!"

I laid my knife and fork down and leaned back in my
chair. My head swam. After a while, when sufficiently
recovered to speak in a steady voice, I instructed my
mate to put the ship round at eight o'clock himself.

"I won't come on deck," I went on. "I think I'll
turn in, and unless the wind shifts I don't want to be
disturbed before midnight. I feel a bit seedy."

"You did look middling bad a little while ago," the
chief mate remarked without showing any great
concern.

They both went out, and I stared at the steward
clearing the table. There was nothing to be read on
that wretched man's face. But why did he avoid my
eyes, I asked myself. Then I thought I should like to
hear the sound of his voice.

"Steward!"

"Sir!" Startled as usual.

"Where did you hang up that coat?"

"In the bathroom, sir." The usual anxious tone. "It's
not quite dry yet, sir."

For some time longer I sat in the cuddy. Had my
double vanished as he had come? But of his coming
there was an explanation, whereas his disappearance
would be inexplicable. . . . I went slowly into my dark
room, shut the door, lighted the lamp, and for a time
dared not turn round. When at last I did I saw him
standing bolt-upright in the narrow recessed part. It
would not be true to say I had a shock, but an irresistible doubt of his bodily existence flitted through my
mind. Can it be, I asked myself, that he is not visible

to other eyes than mine? It was like being haunted.
Motionless, with a grave face, he raised his hands
slightly at me in a gesture which meant clearly, "Heavens! what a narrow escape!" Narrow indeed. I think
I had come creeping quietly as near insanity as any
man who has not actually gone over the border. That
gesture restrained me, so to speak.

The mate with the terrific whiskers was not putting
the ship on the other tack. In the moment of profound
silence which follows upon the hands going to their
stations I heard on the poop his raised voice: "Hard
alee!" and the distant shout of the order repeated on
the main-deck. The sails, in that light breeze, made
but a faint fluttering noise. It ceased. The ship was
coming round slowly: I held my breath in the renewed
stillness of expectation; one wouldn't have thought
that there was a single living soul on her decks. A
sudden brisk shout, "Mainsail haul!" broke the spell,
and in the noisy cries and rush overhead of the men
running away with the main brace we two, down in
my cabin, came together in our usual position by the
bed place.

He did not wait for my question. "I heard him fum-
bling here and just managed to squat myself down in
the bath," he whispered to me. "The fellow only
opened the door and put his arm in to hang the coat
up. All the same——"

"I never thought of that," I whispered back, even
more appalled than before at the closeness of the
shave, and marveling at that something unyielding in
his character which was carrying him through so finely.
There was no agitation in his whisper. Whoever was
being driven distracted, it was not he. He was sane.
And the proof of his sanity was continued when he
took up the whispering again.

"It would never do for me to come to life again."

It was something that a ghost might have said. But
what he was alluding to was his old captain's reluctant
admission of the theory of suicide. It would obviously
serve his turn—if I had understood at all the view

which seemed to govern the unalterable purpose of his action.

"You must maroon me as soon as ever you can get amongst these islands off the Cambodge shore," he went on.

"Maroon you! We are not living in a boy's adventure tale," I protested. His scornful whispering took me up.

"We aren't indeed! There's nothing of a boy's tale in this. But there's nothing else for it. I want no more. You don't suppose I am afraid of what can be done to me? Prison or gallows or whatever they may please. But you don't see me coming back to explain such things to an old fellow in a wig and twelve respectable tradesmen, do you? What can they know whether I am guilty or not—or of *what* I am guilty, either? That's my affair. What does the Bible say? 'Driven off the face of the earth.' Very well, I am off the face of the earth now. As I came at night so I shall go."

"Impossible!" I murmured. "You can't."

"Can't? . . . Not naked like a soul on the Day of Judgment. I shall freeze on to this sleeping suit. The Last Day is not yet—and . . . you have understood thoroughly. Didn't you?"

I felt suddenly ashamed of myself. I may say truly that I understood—and my hesitation in letting that man swim away from my ship's side had been a mere sham sentiment, a sort of cowardice.

"It can't be done now till next night," I breathed out. "The ship is on the off-shore tack and the wind may fail us."

"As long as I know that you understand," he whispered. "But of course you do. It's a great satisfaction to have got somebody to understand. You seem to have been there on purpose." And in the same whisper, as if we two whenever we talked had to say things to each other which were not fit for the world to hear, he added, "It's very wonderful."

We remained side by side talking in our secret way—but sometimes silent or just exchanging a whispered word or two at long intervals. And as usual he stared through the port. A breath of wind came now and again into our faces. The ship might have been moored in dock, so gently and on an even keel she slipped through the water, that did not murmur even at our passage, shadowy and silent like a phantom sea.

At midnight I went on deck, and to my mate's great surprise put the ship round on the other tack. His terrible whiskers flitted round me in silent criticism. I certainly should not have done it if it had been only a question of getting out of that sleepy gulf as quickly as possible. I believe he told the second mate, who relieved him, that it was a great want of judgment. The other only yawned. That intolerable cub shuffled about so sleepily and lolled against the rails in such a slack, improper fashion that I came down on him sharply.

"Aren't you properly awake yet?"

"Yes, sir! I am awake."

"Well, then, be good enough to hold yourself as if you were. And keep a lookout. If there's any current we'll be closing with some islands before daylight."

The east side of the gulf is fringed with islands, some solitary, others in groups. On the blue background of the high coast they seem to float on silvery patches of calm water, arid and gray, or dark green and rounded like clumps of evergreen bushes, with the larger ones, a mile or two long, showing the outlines of ridges, ribs of gray rock under the dank mantle of matted leafage. Unknown to trade, to travel, almost to geography, the manner of life they harbor is an unsolved secret. There must be villages—settlements of fishermen at least—on the largest of them, and some communication with the world is probably kept up by native craft. But all that forenoon, as we headed for them, fanned along by the faintest of breezes, I saw no sign of man or canoe in the field of the telescope I kept on pointing at the scattered group.

At noon I gave no orders for a change of course, and the mate's whiskers became much concerned and seemed to be offering themselves unduly to my notice. At last I said:

"I am going to stand right in. Quite in—as far as I can take her."

The stare of extreme surprise imparted an air of ferocity also to his eyes, and he looked truly terrific for a moment.

"We're not doing well in the middle of the gulf," I continued, casually. "I am going to look for the land breezes tonight."

"Bless my soul! Do you mean, sir, in the dark amongst the lot of all them islands and reefs and shoals?"

"Well—if there are any regular land breezes at all on this coast one must get close inshore to find them, mustn't one?"

"Bless my soul!" he exclaimed again under his breath. All that afternoon he wore a dreamy, contemplative appearance which in him was a mark of perplexity. After dinner I went into my stateroom as if I meant to take some rest. There we two bent our dark heads over a half-unrolled chart lying on my bed.

"There," I said. "It's got to be Koh-ring. I've been looking at it ever since sunrise. It has got two hills and a low point. It must be inhabited. And on the coast opposite there is what looks like the mouth of a biggish river—with some towns, no doubt, not far up. It's the best chance for you that I can see."

"Anything. Koh-ring let it be."

He looked thoughtfully at the chart as if surveying chances and distances from a lofty height—and following with his eyes his own figure wandering on the blank land of Cochin-China, and then passing off that piece of paper clean out of sight into uncharted regions. And it was as if the ship had two captains to plan her course for her. I had been so worried and restless running up and down that I had not had the patience to dress that day. I had remained in my sleeping suit, with straw slippers and a soft floppy hat. The closeness of the heat in the gulf had been most oppressive, and the crew were used to seeing me wandering in that airy attire.

"She will clear the south point as she heads now," I whispered into his ear. "Goodness only knows when, though, but certainly after dark. I'll edge her in to half a mile, as far as I may be able to judge in the dark——"

"Be careful," he murmured, warningly—and I realized suddenly that all my future, the only future for which I was fit, would perhaps go irretrievably to pieces in any mishap to my first command.

I could not stop a moment longer in the room. I motioned him to get out of sight and made my way on the poop. That unplayful cub had the watch. I walked up and down for a while thinking things out, then beckoned him over.

"Send a couple of hands to open the two quarter-deck ports," I said, mildly.

He actually had the impudence, or else so forgot himself in his wonder at such an incomprehensible order, as to repeat:

"Open the quarter-deck ports! What for, sir?"

"The only reason you need concern yourself about is because I tell you to do so. Have them open wide and fastened properly."

He reddened and went off, but I believe made some jeering remark to the carpenter as to the sensible practice of ventilating a ship's quarter-deck. I know he popped into the mate's cabin to impart the fact to him because the whiskers came on deck, as it were by chance, and stole glances at me from below—for signs of lunacy or drunkenness, I suppose.

A little before supper, feeling more restless than ever, I rejoined, for a moment, my second self. And to find him sitting so quietly was surprising, like something against nature, inhuman.

I developed my plan in a hurried whisper.

"I shall stand in as close as I dare and then put her round. I will presently find means to smuggle you out

of here into the sail locker, which communicates with
the lobby. But there is an opening, a sort of square
for hauling the sails out, which gives straight on the
quarter-deck and which is never closed in fine
weather, so as to give air to the sails. When the ship's
way is deadened in stays and all the hands are aft at
the main braces you will have a clear road to slip out
and get overboard through the open quarter-deck
port. I've had them both fastened up. Use a rope's
end to lower yourself into the water so as to avoid a
splash—you know. It could be heard and cause some
beastly complication."

He kept silent for a while, then whispered, "I
understand."

"I won't be there to see you go," I began with an
effort. "The rest . . . I only hope I have understood,
too."

"You have. From first to last"—and for the first
time there seemed to be a faltering, something
strained in his whisper. He caught hold of my arm,
but the ringing of the supper bell made me start. He
didn't though; he only released his grip.

After supper I didn't come below again till well past
eight o'clock. The faint, steady breeze was loaded with
dew; and the wet, darkened sails held all there was of
propelling power in it. The night, clear and starry,
sparkled darkly, and the opaque, lightless patches
shifting slowly against the low stars were the drifting
islets. On the port bow there was a big one more
distant and shadowily imposing by the great space of
sky it eclipsed.

On opening the door I had a back view of my very
own self looking at a chart. He had come out of the
recess and was standing near the table.

"Quite dark enough," I whispered.

He stepped back and leaned against my bed with a
level, quiet glance. I sat on the couch. We had nothing
to say to each other. Over our heads the officer of the
watch moved here and there. Then I heard him move

quickly. I knew what that meant. He was making for the companion; and presently his voice was outside my door.

"We are drawing in pretty fast, sir. Land looks rather close."

"Very well," I answered. "I am coming on deck directly."

I waited till he was gone out of the cuddy, then rose. My double moved too. The time had come to exchange our last whispers, for neither of us was ever to hear each other's natural voice.

"Look here!" I opened a drawer and took out three sovereigns. "Take this anyhow. I've got six and I'd give you the lot, only I must keep a little money to buy some fruit and vegetables for the crew from native boats as we go through Sunda Straits."

He shook his head.

"Take it," I urged him, whispering desperately. "No one can tell what——"

He smiled and slapped meaningly the only pocket of the sleeping jacket. It was not safe, certainly. But I produced a large old silk handkerchief of mine, and tying the three pieces of gold in a corner, pressed it on him. He was touched, I supposed, because he took it at last and tied it quickly round his waist under the jacket, on his bare skin.

Our eyes met; several seconds elapsed, till, our glances still mingled, I extended my hand and turned the lamp out. Then I passed through the cuddy, leaving the door of my room wide open. . . . . "Steward!"

He was still lingering in the pantry in the greatness of his zeal, giving a rub-up to a plated cruet stand the last thing before going to bed. Being careful not to wake up the mate, whose room was opposite, I spoke in an undertone.

He looked round anxiously. "Sir!"

"Can you get me a little hot water from the galley?"

"I am afraid, sir, the galley fire's been out for some time now."

"Go and see."

He flew up the stairs.

"Now," I whispered, loudly, into the saloon—too loudly, perhaps, but I was afraid I couldn't make a sound. He was by my side in an instant—the double captain slipped past the stairs—through a tiny dark passage . . . a sliding door. We were in the sail locker, scrambling on our knees over the sails. A sudden thought struck me. I saw myself wandering barefooted, bareheaded, the sun beating on my dark poll. I snatched off my floppy hat and tried hurriedly in the dark to ram it on my other self. He dodged and fended off silently. I wonder what he thought had come to me before he understood and suddenly desisted. Our hands met gropingly, lingered united in a steady, motionless clasp for a second. . . . No word was breathed by either of us when they separated.

I was standing quietly by the pantry door when the steward returned.

"Sorry, sir. Kettle barely warm. Shall I light the spirit lamp?"

"Never mind."

I came out on deck slowly. It was now a matter of conscience to shave the land as close as possible—for now he must go overboard whenever the ship was put in stays. Must! There could be no going back for him. After a moment I walked over to leeward and my heart flew into my mouth at the nearness of the land on the bow. Under any other circumstances I would not have held on a minute longer. The second mate had followed me anxiously.

I looked on till I felt I could command my voice.

"She will weather," I said then in a quiet tone.

"Are you going to try that, sir?" he stammered out incredulously.

I took no notice of him and raised my tone just enough to be heard by the helmsman.

"Keep her good full."

"Good full, sir."

The wind fanned my cheek, the sails slept, the world was silent. The strain of watching the dark loom of the land grow bigger and denser was too much for me. I had shut my eyes—because the ship must go closer. She must! The stillness was intolerable. Were we standing still?

When I opened my eyes the second view started my heart with a thump. The black southern hill of Koh-ring seemed to hang right over the ship like a towering fragment of the ever-lasting night. On that enormous mass of blackness there was not a gleam to be seen, not a sound to be heard. It was gliding irresistibly towards us and yet seemed already within reach of the hand. I saw the vague figures of the watch grouped in the waist, gazing in awed silence.

"Are you going on, sir?" inquired an unsteady voice at my elbow.

I ignored it. I had to go on.

"Keep her full. Don't check her way. That won't do now," I said, warningly.

"I can't see the sails very well," the helmsman answered me, in strange, quavering tones.

Was she close enough? Already she was, I won't say in the shadow of the land, but in the very blackness of it, already swallowed up as it were, gone too close to be recalled, gone from me altogether.

"Give the mate a call," I said to the young man who stood at my elbow as still as death. "And turn all hands up."

My tone had a borrowed loudness reverberated from the height of the land. Several voices cried out together: "We are all on deck, sir."

Then stillness again, with the great shadow gliding closer, towering higher, without a light, without a sound. Such a hush had fallen on the ship that she might have been a bark of the dead floating in slowly under the very gate of Erebus.

"My God! Where are we?"

It was the mate moaning at my elbow. He was thunder-struck, and as it were deprived of the moral support of his whiskers. He clapped his hands and absolutely cried out, "Lost!"

"Be quiet," I said, sternly.

He lowered his tone, but I saw the shadowy gesture of his despair. "What are we doing here?"

"Looking for the land wind."

He made as if to tear his hair, and addressed me recklessly.

"She will never get out. You have done it, sir. I knew it'd end in something like this. She will never weather, and you are too close now to stay. She'll drift ashore before she's round. O my God!"

I caught his arm as he was raising it to batter his poor devoted head, and shook it violently.

"She's ashore already," he wailed, trying to tear himself away.

"Is she? . . . Keep good full there!"

"Good full, sir," cried the helmsman in a frightened, thin, childlike voice.

I hadn't let go the mate's arm and went on shaking it. "Ready about, do you hear? You go forward"—shake—"and stop there"—shake—"and hold your noise"—shake—"and see these head-sheets properly overhauled"—shake, shake—shake.

And all the time I dared not look towards the land lest my heart should fail me. I released my grip at last and he ran forward as if fleeing for dear life.

I wondered what my double there in the sail locker thought of this commotion. He was able to hear everything—and perhaps he was able to understand why, on my conscience, it had to be thus close—no less. My first order "Hard alee!" re-echoed ominously under the towering shadow of Koh-ring as if I had shouted in a mountain gorge. And then I watched the land intently. In that smooth water and light wind it was impossible to feel the ship coming-to. No! I could not feel her. And my second self was making now ready to ship out and lower himself overboard. Perhaps he was gone already . . . ?

The great black mass brooding over our very mastheads began to pivot away from the ship's side silently. And now I forgot the secret stranger ready to depart,

and remembered only that I was a total stranger to
the ship. I did not know her. Would she do it? How
was she to be handled?

I swung the mainyard and waited helplessly. She
was perhaps stopped, and her very fate hung in the
balance, with the black mass of Koh-ring like the gate
of the everlasting night towering over her taffrail.
What would she do now? Had she way on her yet? I
stepped to the side swiftly, and on the shadowy water
I could see nothing except a faint phosphorescent flash
revealing the glassy smoothness of the sleeping surface. It was impossible to tell—and I had not learned
yet the feel of my ship. Was she moving? What I
needed was something easily seen, a piece of paper,
which I could throw overboard and watch. I had nothing on me. To run down for it I didn't dare. There
was no time. All at once my strained, yearning stare
distinguished a white object floating within a yard of
the ship's side. White on the black water. A phosphorescent flash passed under it. What was that thing? . . .
I recognized my own floppy hat. It must have fallen
off his head . . . and he didn't bother. Now I had what
I wanted—the saving mark for my eyes. But I hardly
thought of my other self, now gone from the ship, to
be hidden forever from all friendly faces, to be a fugitive and a vagabond on the earth, with no brand of
the curse on his sane forehead to stay a slaying
hand . . . too proud to explain.

And I watched the hat—the expression of my sudden pity for his mere flesh. It had been meant to save
his homeless head from the dangers of the sun. And
now—behold—it was saving the ship, by serving me
for a mark to help out the ignorance of my strangeness. Ha! It was drifting forward, warning me just in
time that the ship had gathered sternway.

"Shift the helm," I said in a low voice to the seaman
standing still like a statue.

The man's eyes glistened wildly in the binnacle light
as he jumped round to the other side and spun round
the wheel.

I walked to the break of the poop. On the over-shadowed deck all hands stood by the forebraces waiting for my order. The stars ahead seemed to be gliding from right to left. And all was so still in the world that I heard the quiet remark, "She's round," passed in a tone of intense relief between two seamen.

"Let go and haul."

The foreyards ran round with a great noise, amidst cheery cries. And now the frightful whiskers made themselves heard giving various orders. Already the ship was drawing ahead. And I was alone with her. Nothing! no one in the world should stand now between us, throwing a shadow on the way of silent knowledge and mute affection, the perfect communion of a seaman with his first command.

Walking to the taffrail, I was in time to make out, on the very edge of a darkness thrown by a towering black mass like the very gateway of Erebus—yes, I was in time to catch an evanescent glimpse of my white hat left behind to mark the spot where the secret sharer of my cabin and of my thoughts, as though he were my second self, had lowered himself into the water to take his punishment: a free man, a proud swimmer striking out for a new destiny.

Heart of Darkness

I

The *Nellie,* a cruising yawl, swung to her anchor without a flutter of the sails, and was at rest. The flood had made, the wind was nearly calm, and being bound down the river, the only thing for it was to come to and wait for the turn of the tide.

The sea-reach of the Thames stretched before us like the beginning of an interminable waterway. In the offing the sea and the sky were welded together without a joint, and in the luminous space the tanned sails of the barges drifting up with the tide seemed to stand still in red clusters of canvas sharply peaked, with gleams of varnished sprits. A haze rested on the low shores that ran out to sea in vanishing flatness. The air was dark above Gravesend, and farther back still seemed condensed into a mournful gloom, brooding motionless over the biggest, and the greatest, town on earth.

The Director of Companies was our captain and our host. We four affectionately watched his back as he stood in the bows looking to seaward. On the whole river there was nothing that looked half so nautical. He resembled a pilot, which to a seaman is trustworthiness personified. It was difficult to realize his work was not out there in the luminous estuary, but behind him, within the brooding gloom.

Between us there was, as I have already said somewhere, the bond of the sea. Besides holding our hearts together through long periods of separation, it had the

effect of making us tolerant of each other's yarns—
and even convictions. The Lawyer—the best of old
fellows—had, because of his many years and many
virtues, the only cushion on deck, and was lying on
the only rug. The Accountant had brought out already
a box of dominoes, and was toying architecturally with
the bones. Marlow sat cross-legged right aft, leaning
against the mizzen-mast. He had sunken cheeks, a yellow complexion, a straight back, an ascetic aspect, and,
with his arms dropped, the palms of hands outwards,
resembled an idol. The director, satisfied the anchor
had good hold, made his way aft and sat down
amongst us. We exchanged a few words lazily. Afterwards there was silence on board the yacht. For some
reason or other we did not begin that game of dominoes. We felt meditative, and fit for nothing but placid
staring. The day was ending in a serenity of still and
exquisite brilliance. The water shone pacifically; the
sky, without a speck, was a benign immensity of un-
stained light; the very mist on the Essex marsh was
like a gauzy and radiant fabric, hung from the wooded
rises inland, and draping the low shores in diaphanous
folds. Only the gloom to the west, brooding over the
upper reaches, became more sombre every minute, as
if angered by the approach of the sun.

And at last, in its curved and imperceptible fall, the
sun sank low, and from glowing white changed to a
dull red without rays and without heat, as if about to
go out suddenly, stricken to death by the touch of that
gloom brooding over a crowd of men.

Forthwith a change came over the waters, and the
serenity became less brilliant but more profound. The
old river in its broad reach rested unruffled at the de-
cline of day, after ages of good service done to the
race that peopled its banks, spread out in the tranquil
dignity of a waterway leading to the uttermost ends
of the earth. We looked at the venerable stream not
in the vivid flush of a short day that comes and departs
for ever, but in the august light of abiding memories.
And indeed nothing is easier for a man who has, as

the phrase goes, "followed the sea" with reverence
and affection, than to evoke the great spirit of the
past upon the lower reaches of the Thames. The tidal
current runs to and fro in its unceasing service,
crowded with memories of men and ships it had borne
to the rest of home or to the battles of the sea. It had
known and served all the men of whom the nation is
proud, from Sir Francis Drake to Sir John Franklin,
knights all, titled and untitled—the great knights-
errant of the sea. It had borne all the ships whose
names are like jewels flashing in the night of time,
from the *Golden Hind* returning with her round flanks
full of treasure, to be visited by the Queen's Highness
and thus pass out of the gigantic tale, to the *Erebus*
and *Terror,* bound on other conquests—and that never
returned. It had known the ships and the men. They
had sailed from Deptford, from Greenwich, from
Erith—the adventurers and the settlers; kings' ships
and the ships of men on 'Change; captains, admirals,
the dark "interlopers" of the Eastern trade, and the
commissioned "generals" of East India fleets. Hunters
for gold or pursuers of fame, they all had gone out
on that stream, bearing the sword, and often the torch,
messengers of the might within the land, bearers of a
spark from the sacred fire. What greatness had not
floated on the ebb of that river into the mystery of an
unknown earth! . . . The dreams of men, the seed of
commonwealths, the germs of empires.

The sun set; the dusk fell on the stream, and lights
began to appear along the shore. The Chapman light-
house, a three-legged thing erect on a mud-flat, shone
strongly. Lights of ships moved in the fairway—a great
stir of lights going up and going down. And further
west on the upper reaches the place of the monstrous
town was still marked ominously on the sky, a brooding gloom in sunshine, a lurid glare under the stars.

"And this also," said Marlow suddenly, "has been
one of the dark places of the earth."

He was the only man of us who still "followed the
sea." The worst that could be said of him was that he

did not represent his class. He was a seaman, but he
was a wanderer, too, while most seamen lead, if one
may so express it, a sedentary life. Their minds are of
the stay-at-home order, and their home is always with
them—the ship; and so is their country—the sea. One
ship is very much like another, and the sea is always
the same. In the immutability of their surroundings
the foreign shores, the foreign faces, the changing immensity of life, glide past, veiled not by a sense of
mystery but by a slightly disdainful ignorance; for
there is nothing mysterious to a seaman unless it be
the sea itself, which is the mistress of his existence
and as inscrutable as Destiny. For the rest, after his
hours of work, a casual stroll or a casual spree on
shore suffices to unfold for him the secret of a whole
continent, and generally he finds the secret not worth
knowing. The yarns of seamen have a direct simplicity,
the whole meaning of which lies within the shell of a
cracked nut. But Marlow was not typical (if his propensity to spin yarns be excepted), and to him the
meaning of an episode was not inside like a kernel
but outside, enveloping the tale which brought it out
only as a glow brings out a haze, in the likeness of
one of these misty halos that sometimes are made visible by the spectral illumination of moonshine.

His remark did not seem at all surprising. It was
just like Marlow. It was accepted in silence. No one
took the trouble to grunt even; and presently he said,
very slow—

"I was thinking of very old times, when the Romans
first came here, nineteen hundred years ago—the
other day. . . . Light came out of this river since—you
say knights? Yes; but it is like a running blaze on a
plain, like a flash of lightning in the clouds. We live
in the flicker—may it last as long as the old earth
keeps rolling! But darkness was here yesterday. Imagine the feelings of a commander of a fine—what d'ye
call 'em?—trireme in the Mediterranean, ordered suddenly to the north; run overland across the Gauls in
a hurry; put in charge of one of these craft the

legionaries—a wonderful lot of handy men they must
have been, too—used to build, apparently by the hundred, in a month or two, if we may believe what we
read. Imagine him here—the very end of the world, a
sea the colour of lead, a sky the colour of smoke, a
kind of ship about as rigid as a concertina—and going
up this river with stores, or orders, or what you like.
Sand-banks, marshes, forests, savages,—precious little
to eat fit for a civilized man, nothing but Thames
water to drink. No Falernian wine here, no going
ashore. Here and there a military camp lost in the
wilderness, like a needle in a bundle of hay—cold, fog,
tempests, disease, exile, and death—death skulking in
the air, in the water, in the bush. They must have
been dying like flies here. Oh, yes—he did it. Did it
very well, too, no doubt, and without thinking much
about it either, except afterwards to brag of what he
had gone through in his time, perhaps. They were men
enough to face the darkness. And perhaps he was
cheered by keeping his eye on a chance of promotion
to the fleet at Ravenna by and by, if he had good
friends in Rome and survived the awful climate. Or
think of a decent young citizen in a toga—perhaps too
much dice, you know—coming out here in the train
of some prefect, or tax-gatherer, or trader even, to
mend his fortunes. Land in a swamp, march through
the woods, and in some inland post feel the savagery,
the utter savagery, had closed round him—all that
mysterious life of the wilderness that stirs in the forest,
in the jungles, in the hearts of wild men. There's no
initiation either into such mysteries. He has to live
in the midst of the incomprehensible, which is also
detestable. And it has a fascination, too, that goes to
work upon him. The fascination of the abomination—
you know, imagine the growing regrets, the longing to
escape, the powerless disgust, the surrender, the hate."

He paused.

"Mind," he began again, lifting one arm from the
elbow, the palm of the hand outwards, so that, with his
legs folded before him, he had the pose of a Buddha

preaching in European clothes and without a lotus-
flower—"Mind, none of us would feel exactly like this.
What saves us is efficiency—the devotion to efficiency.
But these chaps were not much account, really. They
were no colonists; their administration was merely a
squeeze, and nothing more, I suspect. They were con-
querors, and for that you want only brute force—
nothing to boast of, when you have it, since your
strength is just an accident arising from the weakness
of others. They grabbed what they could get for the
sake of what was to be got. It was just robbery with
violence, aggravated murder on a great scale, and men
going at it blind—as is very proper for those who
tackle a darkness. The conquest of the earth, which
mostly means the taking it away from those who have
a different complexion or slightly flatter noses than
ourselves, is not a pretty thing when you look into it
too much. What redeems it is the idea only. An idea
at the back of it; not a sentimental pretence but an
idea; and an unselfish belief in the idea—something
you can set up, and bow down before, and offer a
sacrifice to. . . ."

He broke off. Flames glided in the river, small green
flames, red flames, white flames, pursuing, overtaking,
joining, crossing each other—then separating slowly or
hastily. The traffic of the great city went on in the
deepening night upon the sleepless river. We looked
on, waiting patiently—there was nothing else to do till
the end of the flood; but it was only after a long silence, when he said, in a hesitating voice, "I suppose
you fellows remember I did once turn fresh-water
sailor for a bit," that we knew we were fated, before
the ebb began to run, to hear about one of Marlow's
inconclusive experiences.

"I don't want to bother you much with what happened to me personally," he began, showing in this
remark the weakness of many tellers of tales who
seem so often unaware of what their audience would
best like to hear; "yet to understand the effect of it
on me you ought to know how I got out there, what

I saw, how I went up that river to the place where I first met the poor chap. It was the farthest point of navigation and the culminating point of my experience. It seemed somehow to throw a kind of light on everything about me—and into my thoughts. It was sombre enough, too—and pitiful—not extraordinary in any way—not very clear either. No, not very clear. And yet it seemed to throw a kind of light.

"I had then, as you remember, just returned to London after a lot of Indian Ocean, Pacific, China Seas— a regular dose of the East—six years or so, and I was loafing about, hindering you fellows in your work and invading your homes, just as though I had got a heavenly mission to civilize you. It was very fine for a time, but after a bit I did get tired of resting. Then I began to look for a ship—I should think the hardest work on earth. But the ships wouldn't even look at me. And I got tired of that game, too.

"Now when I was a little chap I had a passion for maps. I would look for hours at South America, or Africa, or Australia, and lose myself in all the glories of exploration. At that time there were many blank spaces on the earth, and when I saw one that looked particularly inviting on a map (but they all look that) I would put my finger on it and say, 'When I grow up I will go there.' The North Pole was one of these places, I remember. Well, I haven't been there yet, and shall not try now. The glamour's off. Other places were scattered about the Equator, and in every sort of latitude all over the two hemispheres. I have been in some of them, and . . . well we won't talk about that. But there was one yet—the biggest, the most blank, so to speak—that I had a hankering after.

"True, by this time it was not a blank space any more. It had got filled since my boyhood with rivers and lakes and names. It had ceased to be a blank space of delightful mystery—a white patch for a boy to dream gloriously over. It had become a place of darkness. But there was in it one river especially, a mighty big river, that you could see on the map, resembling an immense snake uncoiled, with its head in the sea, its body at rest curving afar over a vast country, and its tail lost in the depths of the land. And as I looked at the map of it in a shop-window, it fascinated me as a snake would a bird—a silly little bird. Then I remembered there was a big concern, a Company for trade on that river. Dash it all! I thought to myself, they can't trade without using some kind of craft on that lot of fresh water—steamboats! Why shouldn't I try to get charge of one? I went on along Fleet Street, but could not shake off the idea. The snake had charmed me.

"You understand it was a Continental concern, that Trading society; but I have a lot of relations living on the Continent, because it's cheap and not so nasty as it looks, they say.

"I am sorry to own I began to worry them. This was already a fresh departure for me. I was not used to get things that way, you know. I always went my own road and on my own legs where I had a mind to go. I wouldn't have believed it of myself; but, then—you see—I felt somehow I must get there by hook or by crook. So I worried them. The men said 'My dear fellow,' and did nothing. Then—would you believe it?—I tried the women. I, Charlie Marlow, set the women to work—to get a job. Heavens! Well, you see, the notion drove me. I had an aunt, a dear enthusiastic soul. She wrote: 'It will be delightful. I am ready to do anything, anything for you. It is a glorious idea. I know the wife of a very high personage in the Administration, and also a man who has lots of influence with,' etc., etc. She was determined to make no end of fuss to get me appointed skipper of a river steamboat, if such was my fancy.

"I got my appointment—of course; and I got it very quick. It appears the Company had received news that one of their captains had been killed in a scuffle with the natives. This was my chance, and it made me the more anxious to go. It was only months and months afterwards, when I made the attempt to recover what was left of the body, that I heard the original quarrel arose from a misunderstanding about some hens. Yes, two black hens. Fresleven—that was the fellow's name, a Dane—thought himself wronged somehow in the bargain, so he went ashore and started to hammer the chief of the village with a stick. Oh, it didn't surprise me in the least to hear this, and at the same time to be told that Fresleven was the gentlest, quietest creature that ever walked on two legs. No doubt he was; but he had been a couple of years already out there engaged in the noble cause, you know, and he probably felt the need at last of asserting his self-respect in some way. Therefore he whacked the old nigger mercilessly, while a big crowd of his people watched him, thunderstruck, till some man—I was told the chief's son—in desperation at hearing the old chap yell, made a tentative jab with a spear at the white man—and of course it went quite easy between the shoulderblades. Then the whole population cleared into the forest, expecting all kinds of calamities to happen, while, on the other hand, the steamer Fresleven commanded left also in a bad panic, in charge of the engineer, I believe. Afterwards nobody seemed to trouble much about Fresleven's remains, till I got out and stepped into his shoes. I couldn't let it rest, though; but when an opportunity offered at last to meet my predecessor, the grass growing through his ribs was tall enough to hide his bones. They were all there. The supernatural being had not been touched after he fell. And the village was deserted, the huts gaped black, rotting, all askew within the fallen enclosures. A calamity had come to it, sure enough. The people had vanished. Mad terror had scattered them, men, women, and children, through the bush, and they had never returned. What became of the hens I don't know either. I should think the cause of progress got them, anyhow. However, through this glorious affair I got my appointment, before I had fairly begun to hope for it.

"I flew around like mad to get ready, and before

forty-eight hours I was crossing the Channel to show myself to my employers, and sign the contract. In a very few hours I arrived in a city that always makes me think of a whited sepulchre. Prejudice no doubt. I had no difficulty in finding the Company's offices. It was the biggest thing in the town, and everybody I met was full of it. They were going to run an oversea empire, and make no end of coin by trade.

"A narrow and deserted street in deep shadow, high houses, innumerable windows with venetian blinds, a dead silence, grass sprouting between the stones, imposing carriage archways right and left, immense double doors standing ponderously ajar. I slipped through one of these cracks, went up a swept and ungarnished staircase, as arid as a desert, and opened the first door I came to. Two women, one fat and the other slim, sat on straw-bottomed chairs, knitting black wool. The slim one got up and walked straight at me—still knitting with downcast eyes—and only just as I began to think of getting out of her way, as you would for a somnambulist, stood still, and looked up. Her dress was as plain as an umbrella-cover, and she turned round without a word and preceded me into a waiting-room. I gave my name, and looked about. Deal table in the middle, plain chairs all round the walls, on one end a large shining map, marked with all the colours of a rainbow. There was a vast amount of red—good to see at any time, because one knows that some real work is done in there, a deuce of a lot of blue, a little green, smears of orange, and, on the East Coast, a purple patch, to show where the jolly pioneers of progress drink the jolly lager-beer. However, I wasn't going into any of these. I was going into the yellow. Dead in the centre. And the river was there—fascinating—deadly—like a snake. Ough! A door opened, a white-haired secretarial head, but wearing a compassionate expression, appeared, and a skinny forefinger beckoned me into the sanctuary. Its light was dim, and a heavy writing-desk squatted in the middle. From behind that structure came out an impression of pale plumpness in a frock-coat. The great man himself. He was five feet six, I should judge, and had his grip on the handle-end of ever so many millions. He shook hands, I fancy, murmured vaguely, was satisfied with my French. *Bon voyage.*

"In about forty-five seconds I found myself again in the waiting-room with the compassionate secretary, who, full of desolation and sympathy, made me sign some document. I believe I undertook amongst other things not to disclose any trade secrets. Well, I am not going to.

"I began to feel slightly uneasy. You know I am not used to such ceremonies, and there was something ominous in the atmosphere. It was just as though I had been let into some conspiracy—I don't know—something not quite right; and I was glad to get out. In the outer room the two women knitted black wool feverishly. People were arriving, and the younger one was walking back and forth introducing them. The old one sat on her chair. Her flat cloth slippers were propped up on a foot-warmer, and a cat reposed on her lap. She wore a starched white affair on her head, had a wart on one cheek, and silver-rimmed spectacles hung on the top of her nose. She glanced at me above the glasses. The swift and indifferent placidity of that look troubled me. Two youths with foolish and cheery countenances were being piloted over, and she threw at them the same quick glance of unconcerned wisdom. She seemed to know all about them and about me, too. An eerie feeling came over me. She seemed uncanny and fateful. Often far away there I thought of these two, guarding the door of Darkness, knitting black wool as for a warm pall, one introducing, introducing continuously to the unknown, the other scrutinizing the cheery and foolish faces with unconcerned old eyes. *Ave!* Old knitter of black wool. *Morituri te salutant.* Not many of those she looked at ever saw her again—not half, by a long way.

"There was yet a visit to the doctor. 'A simple formality,' assured me the secretary, with an air of taking

an immense part in all my sorrows. Accordingly a
young chap wearing his hat over the left eyebrow,
some clerk I suppose—there must have been clerks in
the business, though the house was as still as a house
in a city of the dead—came from somewhere up-stairs,
and led me forth. He was shabby and careless, with
inkstains on the sleeves of his jacket, and his cravat
was large and billowy, under a chin shaped like the
toe of an old boot. It was a little too early for the
doctor, so I proposed a drink, and thereupon he developed a vein of joviality. As we sat over our vermouths
he glorified the Company's business, and by and by I
expressed casually my surprise at him not going out
there. He became very cool and collected all at once.
'I am not such a fool as I look, quoth Plato to his
disciples,' he said sententiously, emptied his glass with
great resolution, and we rose.

"The old doctor felt my pulse, evidently thinking of
something else the while. 'Good, good for there,' he
mumbled, and then with a certain eagerness asked me
whether I would let him measure my head. Rather
surprised, I said Yes, when he produced a thing like
calipers and got the dimensions back and front and
every way, taking notes carefully. He was an unshaven
little man in a threadbare coat like a gaberdine, with
his feet in slippers, and I thought him a harmless fool.
'I always ask leave, in the interests of science, to measure the crania of those going out there,' he said. 'And
when they come back, too?' I asked. 'Oh, I never see
them,' he remarked; 'and, moreover, the changes take
place inside, you know.' He smiled, as if at some quiet
joke. 'So you are going out there. Famous. Interesting,
too.' He gave me a searching glance, and made another note. 'Ever any madness in your family?' he
asked, in a matter-of-fact tone. I felt very annoyed. 'Is
that question in the interests of science, too?' 'It would
be,' he said, without taking notice of my irritation,
'interesting for science to watch the mental changes
of individuals, on the spot, but . . .' 'Are you an alien-
ist?' I interrupted. 'Every doctor should be—a little,'

answered that original, imperturbably. 'I have a little theory which you messieurs who go out there must help me to prove. This is my share in the advantages my country shall reap from the possession of such a magnificent dependency. The mere wealth I leave to others. Pardon my questions, but you are the first Englishman coming under my observation . . .' I hastened to assure him I was not in the least typical. 'If I were,' said I, 'I wouldn't be talking like this with you.' 'What you say is rather profound, and probably erroneous,' he said, with a laugh. 'Avoid irritation more than exposure to the sun. Adieu. How do you English say, eh? Good-bye. Ah! Good-bye. Adieu. In the tropics one must before everything keep calm.' . . . He lifted a warning forefinger. . . . *'Du calme, du calme. Adieu.'*

"One thing more remained to do—say good-bye to my excellent aunt. I found her triumphant. I had a cup of tea—the last decent cup of tea for many days—and in a room that most soothingly looked just as you would expect a lady's drawing-room to look, we had a long quiet chat by the fireside. In the course of these confidences it became quite plain to me I had been represented to the wife of the high dignitary, and goodness knows to how many more people besides, as an exceptional and gifted creature—a piece of good fortune for the Company—a man you don't get hold of every day. Good heavens! and I was going to take charge of a two-penny-half-penny river-steamboat with a penny whistle attached! It appeared, however, I was also one of the Workers, with a capital—you know. Something like an emissary of light, something like a lower sort of apostle. There had been a lot of such rot let loose in print and talk just about that time, and the excellent woman, living right in the rush of all that humbug, got carried off her feet. She talked about 'weaning those ignorant millions from their horrid ways,' till, upon my word, she made me quite uncomfortable. I ventured to hint that the Company was run for profit.

"'You forget, dear Charlie, that the labourer is wor-

thy of his hire,' she said, brightly. It's queer how out
of touch with truth women are. They live in a world
of their own, and there has never been anything like
it, and never can be. It is too beautiful altogether, and
if they were to set it up it would go to pieces before
the first sunset. Some confounded fact we men have
been living contentedly with ever since the day of creation would start up and knock the whole thing over.

"After this I got embraced, told to wear flannel, be
sure to write often, and so on—and I left. In the
street—I don't know why—a queer feeling came to
me that I was an imposter. Odd thing that I, who used
to clear out for any part of the world at twenty-four
hours' notice, with less thought than most men give
to the crossing of a street, had a moment—I won't
say of hesitation, but of startled pause, before this
commonplace affair. The best way I can explain it to
you is by saying that, for a second or two, I felt as
though, instead of going to the centre of a continent,
I were about to set off for the centre of the earth.

"I left in a French steamer, and she called in every
blamed port they have out there, for, as far as I could
see, the sole purpose of landing soldiers and custom-
house officers. I watched the coast. Watching a coast
as it slips by the ship is like thinking about an enigma.
There it is before you—smiling, frowning, inviting,
grand, mean, insipid, or savage, and always mute with
an air of whispering, 'Come and find out.' This one
was almost featureless, as if still in the making, with an
aspect of monotonous grimness. The edge of a colossal
jungle, so dark-green as to be almost black, fringed
with white surf, ran straight, like a ruled line, far, far
away along a blue sea whose glitter was blurred by a
creeping mist. The sun was fierce, the land seemed to
glisten and drip with steam. Here and there greyish-
whitish specks showed up clustered inside the white
surf, with a flag flying above them perhaps. Settlements some centuries old, and still no bigger than pin-
heads on the untouched expanse of their background.
We pounded along, stopped, landed soldiers; went on,

landed custom-house clerks to levy toll in what looked like a God-forsaken wilderness, with a tin shed and a flag-pole lost in it; landed more soldiers—to take care of the custom-house clerks, presumably. Some, I heard, got drowned in the surf; but whether they did or not, nobody seemed particularly to care. They were just flung out there, and on we went. Every day the coast looked the same, as though we had not moved; but we passed various places—trading places—with names like Gran' Bassam, Little Popo; names that seemed to belong to some sordid farce acted in front of a sinister back-cloth. The idleness of a passenger, my isolation amongst all these men with whom I had no point of contact, the oily and languid sea, the uniform sombreness of the coast, seemed to keep me away from the truth of things, within the toil of a mournful and senseless delusion. The voice of the surf heard now and then was a positive pleasure, like the speech of a brother. It was something natural, that had its reason, that had a meaning. Now and then a boat from the shore gave one a momentary contact with reality. It was paddled by black fellows. You could see from afar the white of their eyeballs glistening. They shouted, sang; their bodies streamed with perspiration; they had faces like grotesque masks—these chaps; but they had bone, muscle, a wild vitality, an intense energy of movement, that was as natural and true as the surf along their coast. They wanted no excuse for being there. They were a great comfort to look at. For a time I would feel I belonged still to a world of straightforward facts; but the feeling would not last long. Something would turn up to scare it away. Once, I remember, we came upon a man-of-war anchored off the coast. There wasn't even a shed there, and she was shelling the bush. It appears the French had one of their wars going on thereabouts. Her ensign dropped limp like a rag; the muzzles of the long six-inch guns stuck out all over the low hull; the greasy, slimy swell swung her up lazily and let her down, swaying her thin masts. In the empty immensity of earth, sky, and water, there she was, incomprehensible, firing into a continent. Pop, would go one of the six-inch guns; a small flame would dart and vanish, a little white smoke would disappear, a tiny projectile would give a feeble screech—and nothing happened. Nothing could happen. There was a touch of insanity in the proceeding, a sense of lugubrious drollery in the sight; and it was not dissipated by somebody on board assuring me earnestly there was a camp of natives—he called them enemies!—hidden out of sight somewhere.

"We gave her her letters (I heard the men in that lonely ship were dying of fever at the rate of three a day) and went on. We called at some more places with farcical names, where the merry dance of death and trade goes on in a still and earthy atmosphere as of an overheated catacomb; all along the formless coast bordered by dangerous surf, as if Nature herself had tried to ward off intruders; in and out of rivers, streams of death in life, whose banks were rotting into mud, whose waters, thickened into slime, invaded the contorted mangroves, that seemed to writhe at us in the extremity of an impotent despair. Nowhere did we stop long enough to get a particularized impression, but the general sense of vague and oppressive wonder grew upon me. It was like a weary pilgrimage amongst hints for nightmares.

"It was upward of thirty days before I saw the mouth of the big river. We anchored off the seat of the government. But my work would not begin till some two hundred miles farther on. So as soon as I could I made a start for a place thirty miles higher up.

"I had my passage on a little sea-going steamer. Her captain was a Swede, and knowing me for a seaman, invited me on the bridge. He was a young man, lean, fair, and morose, with lanky hair and a shuffling gait. As we left the miserable little wharf, he tossed his head contemptuously at the shore. 'Been living there?' he asked. I said, 'Yes.' 'Fine lot these government chaps—are they not?' he went on, speaking English with great precision and considerable bitterness. 'It is funny what some people will do for a few francs a month. I wonder what becomes of that kind when it goes upcountry?' I said to him I expected to see that soon. 'So-o-o!' he exclaimed. He shuffled athwart, keeping one eye ahead vigilantly. 'Don't be too sure,' he continued. 'The other day I took up a man who hanged himself on the road. He was a Swede, too.' 'Hanged himself! Why, in God's name?' I cried. He kept on looking out watchfully. 'Who knows? The sun too much for him, or the country perhaps.'

"At last we opened a reach. A rocky cliff appeared, mounds of turned-up earth by the shore, houses on a hill, others with iron roofs, amongst a waste of excavations, or hanging to the declivity. A continuous noise of the rapids above hovered over this scene of inhabited devastation. A lot of people, mostly black and naked, moved about like ants. A jetty projected into the river. A blinding sunlight drowned all this at times in a sudden recrudescence of glare. 'There's your Company's station,' said the Swede, pointing to three wooden barrack-like structures on the rocky slope. 'I will send your things up. Four boxes did you say? So. Farewell.'

"I came upon a boiler wallowing in the grass, then found a path leading up the hill. It turned aside for the boulders, and also for an undersized railway-truck lying there on its back with its wheels in the air. One was off. The thing looked as dead as the carcass of some animal. I came upon more pieces of decaying machinery, a stack of rusty rails. To the left a clump of trees made a shady spot, where dark things seemed to stir feebly. I blinked, the path was steep. A horn tooted to the right, and I saw the black people run. A heavy and dull detonation shook the ground, a puff of smoke came out of the cliff, and that was all. No change appeared on the face of the rock. They were building a railway. The cliff was not in the way or anything; but this objectless blasting was all the work going on.

"A slight clinking behind me made me turn my head. Six black men advanced in a file, toiling up the path. They walked erect and slow, balancing small baskets full of earth on their heads, and the clink kept time with their footsteps. Black rags were wound round their loins, and the short ends behind waggled to and fro like tails. I could see every rib, the joints of their limbs were like knots in a rope; each had an iron collar on his neck, and all were connected together with a chain whose bights swung between them, rhythmically clinking. Another report from the cliff made me think suddenly of that ship of war I had seen firing into a continent. It was the same kind of ominous voice; but these men could by no stretch of imagination be called enemies. They were called criminals, and the outraged law, like the bursting shells, had come to them, an insoluble mystery from the sea. All their meagre breasts panted together, the violently dilated nostrils quivered, the eyes stared stonily uphill. They passed me within six inches, without a glance, with that complete, deathlike indifference of unhappy savages. Behind this raw matter one of the reclaimed, the product of the new forces at work, strolled despondently, carrying a rifle by its middle. He had a uniform jacket with one button off, and seeing a white man on the path, hoisted his weapon to his shoulder with alacrity. This was simple prudence, white men being so much alike at a distance that he could not tell who I might be. He was speedily reassured, and with a large, white, rascally grin, and a glance at his charge, seemed to take me into partnership in his exalted trust. After all, I also was a part of the great cause of these high and just proceedings.

"Instead of going up, I turned and descended to the left. My idea was to let that chain-gang get out of sight before I climbed the hill. You know I am not particularly tender; I've had to strike and to fend off. I've had to resist and to attack sometimes—that's only one way of resisting—without counting the exact cost, according to the demands of such sort of life as I had blundered into. I've seen the devil of violence, and the devil of greed, and the devil of hot desire; but, by all the stars! these were strong, lusty, red-eyed devils, that swayed and drove men—men, I tell you. But as I stood on this hillside, I foresaw that in the blinding sunshine of that land I would become acquainted with a flabby, pretending, weak-eyed devil of a rapacious and pitiless folly. How insidious he could be, too, I was only to find out several months later and a thousand miles farther. For a moment I stood appalled, as though by a warning. Finally I descended the hill, obliquely, towards the trees I had seen.

"I avoided a vast artificial hole somebody had been digging on the slope, the purpose of which I found it impossible to divine. It wasn't a quarry or a sandpit, anyhow. It was just a hole. It might have been connected with the philanthropic desire of giving the criminals something to do. I don't know. Then I nearly fell into a very narrow ravine, almost no more than a scar in the hillside. I discovered that a lot of imported drainage-pipes for the settlement had been tumbled in there. There wasn't one that was not broken. It was a wanton smash-up. At last I got under the trees. My purpose was to stroll into the shade for a moment; but no sooner within than it seemed to me I had stepped into the gloomy circle of some Inferno. The rapids were near, and an uninterrupted, uniform, headlong, rushing noise filled the mournful stillness of the grove, where not a breath stirred, not a leaf moved, with a mysterious sound—as though the tearing pace of the launched earth had suddenly become audible.

"Black shapes crouched, lay, sat between the trees leaning against the trunks, clinging to the earth, half coming out, half effaced with the dim light, in all the attitudes of pain, abandonment, and despair. Another mine on the cliff went off, followed by a slight shudder of the soil under my feet. The work was going on. The work! And this was the place where some of the helpers had withdrawn to die.

"They were dying slowly—it was very clear. They were not enemies, they were not criminals, they were nothing earthly, now—nothing but black shadows of disease and starvation, lying confusedly in the greenish gloom. Brought from all the recesses of the coast in all the legality of time contracts, lost in uncongenial surroundings, fed on unfamiliar food, they sickened, became inefficient, and were then allowed to crawl away and rest. These moribund shapes were free as air—and nearly as thin. I began to distinguish the gleam of the eyes under the trees. Then, glancing down, I saw a face near my hand. The black bones reclined at full length with one shoulder against the tree, and slowly the eyelids rose and the sunken eyes looked up at me, enormous and vacant, a kind of blind, white flicker in the depths of the orbs, which died out slowly. The man seemed young—almost a boy—but you know with them it's hard to tell. I found nothing else to do but to offer him one of my good Swede's ship's biscuits I had in my pocket. The fingers closed slowly on it and held—there was no other movement and no other glance. He had tied a bit of white worsted round his neck—Why? Where did he get it? Was it a badge—an ornament—a charm—a propitiatory act? Was there any idea at all connected with it? It looked startling round his black neck, this bit of white thread from beyond the seas.

"Near the same tree two more bundles of acute angles sat with their legs drawn up. One, with his chin propped on his knees, stared at nothing, in an intolerable and appalling manner: his brother phantom rested its forehead, as if overcome with a great weariness; and all about others were scattered in every pose of contorted collapse, as in some picture of a massacre or a pestilence. While I stood horror-struck, one of these creatures rose to his hands and knees, and went off on all-fours towards the river to drink. He lapped out of his hand, then sat up in the sunlight, crossing his shins in front of him, and after a time let his woolly head fall on his breastbone.

"I didn't want any more loitering in the shade, and I made haste towards the station. When near the buildings I met a white man, in such an unexpected elegance of get-up that in the first moment I took him for a sort of vision. I saw a high starched collar, white cuffs, a light alpaca jacket, snowy trousers, a clean necktie, and varnished boots. No hat. Hair parted, brushed, oiled, under a green-lined parasol held in a big white hand. He was amazing, and had a penholder behind his ear.

"I shook hands with this miracle, and I learned he was the Company's chief accountant, and that all the bookkeeping was done at this station. He had come out for a moment, he said, 'to get a breath of fresh air.' The expression sounded wonderfully odd, with its suggestion of sedentary desk-life. I wouldn't have mentioned the fellow to you at all, only it was from his lips that I first heard the name of the man who is so indissolubly connected with the memories of that time. Moreover, I respected the fellow. Yes; I respected his collars, his vast cuffs, his brushed hair. His appearance was certainly that of a hairdresser's dummy; but in the great demoralization of the land he kept up his appearance. That's backbone. His starched collars and got-up shirt-fronts were achievements of character. He had been out nearly three years; and, later, I could not help asking him how he managed to sport such linen. He had just the faintest blush, and said modestly, 'I've been teaching one of the native women about the station. It was difficult. She had a distaste for the work.' Thus this man had verily accomplished something. And he was devoted to his books, which were in apple-pie order.

"Everything else in the station was in a muddle—heads, things, buildings. Strings of dusty niggers with splay feet arrived and departed; a stream of manufactured goods, rubbishy cottons, beads, and brass-wire set into the depths of darkness, and in return came a precious trickle of ivory.

"I had to wait in the station for ten days—an eternity. I lived in a hut in the yard, but to be out of the chaos I would sometimes get into the accountant's office. It was built on horizontal planks, and so badly put together that, as he bent over his high desk, he was barred from neck to heels with narrow strips of sunlight. There was no need to open the big shutter to see. It was hot there, too; big flies buzzed fiendishly, and did not sting, but stabbed. I sat generally on the floor, while, of faultless appearance (and even slightly scented), perching on a high stool, he wrote, he wrote. Sometimes he stood up for exercise. When a truckle-bed with a sick man (some invalid agent from upcountry) was put in there, he exhibited a gentle annoyance. 'The groans of this sick person,' he said, 'distract my attention. And without that it is extremely difficult to guard against clerical errors in this climate.'

"One day he remarked, without lifting his head, 'In the interior you will no doubt meet Mr. Kurtz.' On my asking who Mr. Kurtz was, he said he was a first-class agent; and seeing my disappointment at this information, he added slowly, laying down his pen, 'He is a very remarkable person.' Further questions elicited from him that Mr. Kurtz was at present in charge of a trading-post, a very important one, in the true ivory-country, at 'the very bottom of there. Sends in as much ivory as all the others put together . . .' He began to write again. The sick man was too ill to groan. The flies buzzed in a great peace.

"Suddenly there was a growing murmur of voices and a great tramping of feet. A caravan had come in. A violent babble of uncouth sounds burst out on the other side of the planks. All the carriers were speaking together, and in the midst of the uproar the lamentable voice of the chief agent was heard 'giving it up' tearfully for the twentieth time that day. . . . He rose slowly. 'What a frightful row,' he said. He crossed the room gently to look at the sick man, and returning, said to me, 'He does not hear.' 'What! Dead?' I asked, startled. 'No, not yet,' he answered, with great composure. Then, alluding with a toss of the head to the tumult in the station-yard, 'When one has got to make correct entries, one comes to hate those savages—hate them to the death.' He remained thoughtful for a moment. 'When you see Mr. Kurtz,' he went on, 'tell him from me that everything here'—he glanced at the desk—'is very satisfactory. I don't like to write to him—with those messengers of ours you never know who may get hold of your letter—at that Central Station.' He stared a me for a moment with his mild, bulging eyes. 'Oh, he will go far, very far,' he began again. 'He will be somebody in the Administration before long. They, above—the Council of Europe, you know—mean him to be.'

"He turned to his work. The noise outside had ceased, and presently in going out I stopped at the door. In the steady buzz of flies the homeward-bound agent was lying flushed and insensible; the other, bent over his books, was making correct entries of perfectly correct transactions; and fifty feet below the doorstep I could see the still tree-tops of the grove of death.

"Next day I left that station at last, with a caravan of sixty men, for a two-hundred-mile tramp.

"No use telling you much about that. Paths, paths, everywhere; a stamped-in network of paths spreading over the empty land, through the long grass, through burnt grass, through thickets, down and up chilly ravines, up and down stony hills ablaze with heat; and a solitude, a solitude, nobody, not a hut. The population had cleared out a long time ago. Well, if a lot of mysterious niggers armed with all kinds of fearful weapons suddenly took to travelling on the road between Deal and Gravesend, catching the yokels right and left to carry heavy loads for them, I fancy every farm and cottage thereabouts would get empty very soon. Only here the dwellings were gone, too. Still I passed through several abandoned villages. There's something pathetically childish in the ruins of grass walls. Day after day, with the stamp and shuffle of sixty pair of bare feet behind me, each pair under a 60-lb. load. Camp, cook, sleep, strike camp, march.

Now and then a carrier dead in harness, at rest in the long grass near the path, with an empty water-gourd and his long staff lying by his side. A great silence around and above. Perhaps on some quiet night the tremor of far-off drums, sinking, swelling, a tremor vast, faint; a sound weird, appealing, suggestive, and wild—and perhaps with as profound a meaning as the sound of bells in a Christian country. Once a white man in an unbuttoned uniform, camping on the path with an armed escort of lank Zanzibaris, very hospitable and festive—not to say drunk. Was looking after the upkeep of the road, he declared. Can't say I saw any road or any upkeep, unless the body of a middle-aged negro, with a bullet-hole in the forehead, upon which I absolutely stumbled three miles farther on, may be considered as a permanent improvement. I had a white companion, too, not a bad chap, but rather too fleshy and with the exasperating habit of fainting on the hot hillsides, miles away from the least bit of shade and water. Annoying, you know, to hold your own coat like a parasol over a man's head while he is coming to. I couldn't help asking him once what he meant by coming there at all. 'To make money, of course. What do you think?' he said, scornfully. Then he got fever, and had to be carried in a hammock slung under a pole. As he weighed sixteen stone I had no end of rows with the carriers. They jibbed, ran away, sneaked off with their loads in the night—quite a mutiny. So, one evening, I made a speech in English with gestures, not one of which was lost to the sixty pairs of eyes before me, and the next morning I started the hammock off in front all right. An hour afterwards I came upon the whole concern wrecked in a bush—man, hammock, groans, blankets, horrors. The heavy pole had skinned his poor nose. He was very anxious for me to kill somebody, but there wasn't the shadow of a carrier near. I remembered the old doctor—'It would be interesting for science to watch the mental changes of individuals, on the spot.' I felt I was becoming scientifically interesting. However, all that is to no purpose. On the fifteenth day I came in sight of the big river again, and hobbled into the Central Station. It was on a back water surrounded by scrub and forest, with a pretty border of smelly mud on one side, and on the three others enclosed by a crazy fence of rushes. A neglected gap was all the gate it had, and the first glance at the place was enough to let you see the flabby devil was running that show. White men with long staves in their hands appeared languidly from amongst the buildings, strolling up to take a look at me, and then retired out of sight somewhere. One of them, a stout, excitable chap with black moustaches, informed me with great volubility and many digressions, as soon as I told him who I was, that my steamer was at the bottom of the river. I was thunderstruck. What, how, why? Oh, it was 'all right.' The 'manager himself' was there. All quite correct. 'Everybody had behaved splendidly! splendidly!'— 'you must,' he said in agitation, 'go and see the general manager at once. He is waiting!'

"I did not see the real significance of that wreck at once. I fancy I see it now, but I am not sure—not at all. Certainly the affair was too stupid—when I think of it—to be altogether natural. Still . . . But at the moment it presented itself simply as a confounded nuisance. The steamer was sunk. They had started two days before in a sudden hurry up the river with the manager on board, in charge of some volunteer skipper, and before they had been out three hours they tore the bottom out of her on stones and she sank near the south bank. I asked myself what I was to do there, now my boat was lost. As a matter of fact, I had plenty to do in fishing my command out of the river. I had to set about it the very next day. That, and the repairs when I brought the pieces to the station, took some months.

"My first interview with the manager was curious. He did not ask me to sit down after my twenty-mile walk that morning. He was commonplace in complexion, in feature, in manners, and in voice. He was of

middle size and of ordinary build. His eyes, of the
usual blue, were perhaps remarkably cold, and he certainly could make his glance fall on one as trenchant
and heavy as an axe. But even at these times the rest
of his person seemed to disclaim the intention. Otherwise there was only an indefinable, faint expression of
his lips, something stealthy—a smile—not a smile—I
remember it, but I can't explain. It was unconscious,
this smile was, though just after he had said something
it got intensified for an instant. It came at the end of
his speeches like a seal applied on the words to make
the meaning of the commonest phrase appear absolutely inscrutable. He was a common trader, from his
youth up employed in these parts—nothing more. He
was obeyed, yet he inspired neither love nor fear, nor
even respect. He inspired uneasiness. That was it! Uneasiness. Not a definite mistrust—just uneasiness—
nothing more. You have no idea how effective such
a . . . a . . . faculty can be. He had no genius for
organizing, for initiative, or for order even. That was
evident in such things as the deplorable state of the
station. He had no learning, and no intelligence. His
position had come to him—why? Perhaps because he
was never ill . . . He had served three terms of three
years out there . . . Because triumphant health in the
general rout of constitutions is a kind of power in itself.
When he went home on leave he rioted on a large
scale—pompously. Jack ashore—with a difference—in
externals only. This one could gather from his casual
talk. He originated nothing, he could keep the routine
going—that's all. But he was great. He was great by
this little thing that it was impossible to tell what could
control such a man. He never gave that secret away.
Perhaps there was nothing within him. Such a suspicion made one pause—for out there there were no
external checks. Once when various tropical diseases
had laid low almost every 'agent' in the station, he
was heard to say, 'Men who come out here should
have no entrails.' He sealed the utterance with that
smile of his, as though it had been a door opening

into a darkness he had in his keeping. You fancied you had seen things—but the seal was on. When annoyed at meal-times by the constant quarrels of the white men about precedence, he ordered an immense round table to be made, for which a special house had to be built. This was the station's mess-room. Where he sat was the first place—the rest were nowhere. One felt this to be his unalterable conviction. He was neither civil nor uncivil. He was quiet. He allowed his 'boy'—an overfed young negro from the coast—to treat the white men, under his very eyes, with provoking insolence.

"He began to speak as soon as he saw me. I had been very long on the road. He could not wait. Had to start without me. The up-river stations had to be relieved. There had been so many delays already that he did not know who was dead and who was alive, and how they got on—and so on, and so on. He paid no attention to my explanations, and, playing with a stick of sealing-wax, repeated several times that the situation was 'very grave, very grave.' There were rumours that a very important station was in jeopardy, and its chief, Mr. Kurtz, was ill. Hoped it was not true. Mr. Kurtz was . . . I felt weary and irritable. Hang Kurtz, I thought. I interrupted him by saying I had heard of Mr. Kurtz on the coast. 'Ah! So they talk of him down there,' he murmured to himself. Then he began again, assuring me Mr. Kurtz was the best agent he had, an exceptional man, of the greatest importance to the Company; therefore I could understand his anxiety. He was, he said, 'very, very uneasy.' Certainly he fidgeted on his chair a good deal, exclaimed, 'Ah, Mr. Kurtz!' broke the stick of sealing-wax and seemed dumfounded by the accident. Next thing he wanted to know 'how long it would take to' . . . I interrupted him again. Being hungry, you know, and kept on my feet too, I was getting savage. 'How can I tell?' I said. 'I haven't even seen the wreck yet—some months, no doubt.' All this talk seemed to me so futile. 'Some months,' he said. 'Well, let us say

three months before we can make a start. Yes. That
ought to do the affair.' I flung out of his hut (he lived
all alone in a clay hut with a sort of verandah) mut-
tering to myself my opinion of him. He was a chattering idiot. Afterwards I took it back when it was
borne in upon me startlingly with what extreme nicety
he had estimated the time requisite for the 'affair.'

"I went to work the next day, turning, so to speak,
my back on that station. In that way only it seemed
to me I could keep my hold on the redeeming facts
of life. Still, one must look about sometimes; and then
I saw this station, these men strolling aimlessly about
in the sunshine of the yard. I asked myself sometimes
what it all meant. They wandered here and there with
their absurd long staves in their hands, like a lot of
faithless pilgrims bewitched inside a rotten fence. The
word 'ivory' rang in the air, was whispered, was sighed.
You would think they were praying to it. A taint of
imbecile rapacity blew through it all, like a whiff from
some corpse. By Jove! I've never seen anything so
unreal in my life. And outside, the silent wilderness
surrounding this cleared speck on the earth struck me
as something great and invincible, like evil or truth,
waiting patiently for the passing away of this fantastic invasion.

"Oh, these months! Well, never mind. Various
things happened. One evening a grass shed full of calico, cotton prints, beads, and I don't know what else,
burst into a blaze so suddenly that you would have
thought the earth had opened to let an avenging fire
consume all that trash. I was smoking my pipe quietly
by my dismantled steamer, and saw them all cutting
capers in the light, with their arms lifted high, when
the stout man with moustaches came tearing down to
the river, a tin pail in his hand, assured me that everybody was 'behaving splendidly, splendidly,' dipped
about a quart of water and tore back again. I noticed
there was a hole in the bottom of his pail.

"I strolled up. There was no hurry. You see the
thing had gone off like a box of matches. It had been

hopeless from the very first. The flame had leaped high, driven everybody back, lighted up everything— and collapsed. The shed was already a heap of embers glowing fiercely. A nigger was being beaten near by. They said he had caused the fire in some way; be that as it may, he was screeching most horribly. I saw him, later, for several days, sitting in a bit of shade looking very sick and trying to recover himself: afterwards he arose and went out—and the wilderness without a sound took him into its bosom again. As I approached the glow from the dark I found myself at the back of two men, talking. I heard the name of Kurtz pronounced, then the words, 'take advantage of this unfortunate accident.' One of the men was the manager. I wished him a good evening. 'Did you ever see anything like it—eh? it is incredible,' he said, and walked off. The other man remained. He was a first-class agent, young, gentlemanly, a bit reserved, with a forked little beard and a hooked nose. He was standoffish with the other agents, and they on their side said he was the manager's spy upon them. As to me, I had hardly ever spoken to him before. We got into talk, and by and by we strolled away from the hissing ruins. Then he asked me to his room, which was in the main building of the station. He struck a match, and I perceived that this young aristocrat had not only a silver-mounted dressing-case but also a whole candle all to himself. Just at that time the manager was the only man supposed to have any right to candles. Native mats covered the clay walls; a collection of spears, assegais, shields, knives was hung up in trophies. The business intrusted to this fellow was the making of bricks—so I had been informed; but there wasn't a fragment of a brick anywhere in the station, and he had been there more than a year—waiting. It seems he could not make bricks without something, I don't know what—straw maybe. Anyway, it could not be found there and as it was not likely to be sent from Europe, it did not appear clear to me what he was waiting for. An act of special creation perhaps. How-

ever, they were all waiting—all the sixteen or twenty
pilgrims of them—for something; and upon my word
it did not seem an uncongenial occupation, from the
way they took it, though the only thing that ever came
to them was disease—as far as I could see. They beguiled the time by back-biting and intriguing against
each other in a foolish kind of way. There was an air
of plotting about that station, but nothing came of it,
of course. It was as unreal as everything else—as the
philanthropic pretence of the whole concern, as their
talk, as their government, as their show of work. The
only real feeling was a desire to get appointed to a
trading-post where ivory was to be had, so that they
could earn percentages. They intrigued and slandered
and hated each other only on that account—but as to
effectually lifting a little finger—oh, no. By heavens!
there is something after all in the world allowing one
man to steal a horse while another must not look at
a halter. Steal a horse straight out. Very well. He has
done it. Perhaps he can ride. But there is a way of
looking at a halter that would provoke the most chari-
table of saints into a kick.

"I had no idea why he wanted to be sociable, but
as we chatted in there it suddenly occurred to me the
fellow was trying to get at something—in fact, pump-
ing me. He alluded constantly to Europe, to the people I was supposed to know there—putting leading
questions as to my acquaintances in the sepulchral
city, and so on. His little eyes glittered like mica
discs—with curiosity—though he tried to keep up a
bit of superciliousness. At first I was astonished, but
very soon I became awfully curious to see what he
would find out from me. I couldn't possibly imagine
what I had in me to make it worth his while. It was
very pretty to see how he baffled himself, for in truth
my body was full only of chills, and my head had
nothing in it but that wretched steamboat business.
It was evident he took me for a perfectly shameless
prevaricator. At last he got angry, and, to conceal a
movement of furious annoyance, he yawned. I rose.

Then I noticed a small sketch of oils, on a panel, representing a woman, draped and blindfolded, carrying a lighted torch. The background was sombre—almost black. The movement of the woman was stately, and the effect of the torchlight on the face was sinister.

"It arrested me, and he stood by civilly, holding an empty half-pint champagne bottle (medical comforts) with the candle stuck in it. To my question he said Mr. Kurtz had painted this—in this very station more than a year ago—while waiting for means to go to his trading-post. 'Tell me, pray,' said I, 'who is this Mr. Kurtz?'

" 'The chief of the Inner Station,' he answered in a short tone, looking away. 'Much obliged,' I said, laughing. 'And you are the brickmaker of the Central Station. Every one knows that.' He was silent for a while. 'He is a prodigy,' he said at last. 'He is an emissary of pity and science and progress, and devil knows what else. We want,' he began to declaim suddenly, 'for the guidance of the cause intrusted to us by Europe, so to speak, higher intelligence, wide sympathies, a singleness of purpose.' 'Who says that?' I asked. 'Lots of them,' he replied. 'Some even write that; and so *he* comes here, a special being, as you ought to know.' 'Why ought I to know?' I interrupted, really surprised. He paid no attention. 'Yes. Today he is chief of the best station, next year he will be assistant-manager, two years more and . . . but I daresay you know what he will be in two years' time. You are of the new gang—the gang of virtue. The same people who sent him specially also recommended you. Oh, don't say so. I've my own eyes to trust.' Light dawned upon me. My dear aunt's influential acquaintances were producing an unexpected effect upon that young man. I nearly burst into a laugh. 'Do you read the Company's confidential correspondence?' I asked. He hadn't a word to say. It was great fun. 'When Mr. Kurtz,' I continued, severely, 'is General Manager, you won't have the opportunity.'

"He blew the candle out suddenly, and we went

outside. The moon had risen. Black figures strolled about listlessly, pouring water on the glow, whence proceeded a sound of hissing; steam ascended in the moonlight, the beaten nigger groaned somewhere. 'What a row the brute makes!' said the indefatigable man with the moustaches, appearing near us. 'Serve him right. Transgression—punishment—bang! Pitiless, pitiless. That's the only way. This will prevent all con-flagrations for the future. I was just telling the manager . . .' He noticed my companion, and became crestfallen all at once. 'Not in bed yet,' he said, with a kind of servile heartiness; 'it's so natural. Ha! Danger—agitation.' He vanished. I went on to the riv-erside, and the other followed me. I heard a scathing murmur at my ear. 'Heap of muffs—go to.' The pil-grims could be seen in knots gesticulating, discussing. Several had still their staves in their hands. I verily believe they took these sticks to bed with them. Beyond the fence the forest stood up spectrally in the moonlight, and through the dim stir, through the faint sounds of that lamentable courtyard, the silence of the land went home to one's very heart—its mystery, its greatness, the amazing reality of its concealed life. The hurt nigger moaned feebly somewhere near by, and then fetched a deep sigh that made me mend my pace away from there. I felt a hand introducing itself under my arm. 'My dear sir,' said the fellow, 'I don't want to be misun-derstood, and especially by you, who will see Mr. Kurtz long before I can have that pleasure. I wouldn't like him to get a false idea of my disposition. . . .'

"I let him run on, this papier-mâché Mephisto-pheles, and it seemed to me that if I tried I could poke my forefinger through him, and would find noth-ing inside but a little loose dirt, maybe. He, don't you see, had been planning to be assistant-manager by and by under the present man, and I could see that the coming of that Kurtz had upset them both not a little. He talked precipitately, and I did not try to stop him. I had my shoulders against the wreck of my steamer, hauled up on the slope like a carcass of some big river animal. The smell of mud, of primeval mud, by Jove! was in my nostrils, the high stillness of primeval forest was before my eyes; there were shiny patches on the black creek. The moon had spread over everything a thin layer of silver—over the rank grass, over the mud, upon the wall of matted vegetation standing higher than the wall of a temple, over the great river I could see through a sombre gap glittering, glittering, as it flowed broadly by without a murmur. All this was great, expectant, mute, while the man jabbered about himself. I wondered whether the stillness on the face of the immensity looking at us two were meant as an appeal or as a menace. What were we who had stayed in here? Could we handle that dumb thing, or would it handle us? I felt how big, how confoundedly big, was that thing that couldn't talk, and perhaps was deaf as well. What was in there? I could see a little ivory coming out from there, and I had heard Mr. Kurtz was in there. I had heard enough about it, too—God knows! Yet somehow it didn't bring any image with it—no more than if I had been told an angel or a fiend was in there. I believed it in the same way one of you might believe there are inhabitants in the planet Mars. I knew once a Scotch sailmaker who was certain, dead sure, there were people in Mars. If you asked him for some idea how they looked and behaved, he would get shy and mutter something about 'walking on all-fours.' If you as much as smiled, he would—though a man of sixty—offer to fight you. I would not have gone so far as to fight for Kurtz, but I went for him near enough to a lie. You know I hate, detest, and can't bear a lie, not because I am straighter than the rest of us, but simply because it appalls me. There is a taint of death, a flavour of mortality in lies—which is exactly what I hate and detest of the world—what I want to forget. It makes me miserable and sick, like biting something rotten would do. Temperament, I suppose. Well, I went near enough to it by letting the young fool there believe anything he liked to imagine as to my influence in Europe. I be-

came in an instant as much of a pretence as the rest
of the bewitched pilgrims. This simply because I had
a notion it somehow would be of help to that Kurtz
whom at the time I did not see—you understand. He
was just a word for me. I did not see the man in the
name any more than you do. Do you see him? Do
you see the story? Do you see anything? It seems to
me I am trying to tell you a dream—making a vain
attempt, because no relation of a dream can convey
the dream-sensation, that commingling of absurdity,
surprise, and bewilderment in a tremor of struggling
revolt, that notion of being captured by the incredible
which is of the very essence of dreams. . . ."

He was silent for a while.

". . . No, it is impossible; it is impossible to convey
the life-sensation of any given epoch of one's
existence—that which makes its truth, its meaning—
its subtle and penetrating essence. It is impossible. We
live, as we dream—alone. . . ."

He paused again as if reflecting, then added:

"Of course in this you fellows see more than I could
then. You see me, whom you know. . . ."

It had become so pitch dark that we listeners could
hardly see one another. For a long time already he,
sitting apart, had been no more to us than a voice.
There was not a word from anybody. The others might
have been asleep, but I was awake. I listened, I listened on the watch for the sentence, for the word,
that would give me the clue to the faint uneasiness
inspired by this narrative that seemed to shape itself
without human lips in the heavy night-air of the river.

". . . Yes—I let him run on," Marlow began again,
"and think what he pleased about the powers that
were behind me. I did! And there was nothing behind
me! There was nothing but that wretched, old, man-
gled steamboat I was leaning against, while he talked
fluently about 'the necessity for every man to get on.'
'And when one comes out here, you conceive, it is
not to gaze at the moon.' Mr. Kurtz was a 'universal
genius,' but even a genius would find it easier to work

with 'adequate tools—intelligent men.' He did not make bricks—why, there was a physical impossibility in the way—as I was well aware; and if he did secretarial work for the manager, it was because 'no sensible man rejects wantonly the confidence of his superiors.' Did I see it? I saw it. What more did I want? What I really wanted was rivets, by heaven! Rivets. To get on with the work—to stop the hole. Rivets I wanted. There were cases of them down at the coast—cases—piled up—burst—split! You kicked a loose rivet at every second step in that station-yard on the hillside. Rivets had rolled into the grove of death. You could fill your pockets with rivets for the trouble of stooping down—and there wasn't one rivet to be found where it was wanted. We had plates that would do, but nothing to fasten them with. And every week the messenger, a lone negro, letter-bag on shoulder and staff in hand, left our station for the coast. And several times a week a coast caravan came in with trade goods—ghastly glazed calico that made you shudder only to look at it, glass beads, value about a penny a quart, confounded spotted cotton handkerchiefs. And no rivets. Three carriers could have brought all that was wanted to set that steamboat afloat.

"He was becoming confidential now, but I fancy my unresponsive attitude must have exasperated him at last, for he judged it necessary to inform me he feared neither God nor devil, let alone any mere man. I said I could see that very well, but what I wanted was a certain quantity of rivets—and rivets were what really Mr. Kurtz wanted, if he had only known it. Now letters went to the coast every week. . . . 'My dear sir,' he cried, 'I write from dictation.' I demanded rivets. There was a way—for an intelligent man. He changed his manner; became very cold, and suddenly began to talk about a hippopotamus; wondered whether sleeping on board the steamer (I stuck to my salvage night and day) I wasn't disturbed. There was an old hippo that had the bad habit of getting out on the bank and roaming at night over the station grounds. The pilgrims used to turn out in a body and empty every rifle they could lay hands on at him. Some even had sat up o' nights for him. All this energy was wasted, though. 'That animal has a charmed life,' he said; 'but you can say this only of brutes in this country. No man—you apprehend me?—no man here bears a charmed life.' He stood there for a moment in the moonlight with his delicate hooked nose set a little askew, and his mica eyes glittering without a wink, then, with a curt Good-night, he strode off. I could see he was disturbed and considerably puzzled, which made me feel more hopeful than I had been for days. It was a great comfort to turn from that chap to my influential friend, the battered, twisted, ruined, tin-pot steamboat. I clambered on board. She rang under my feet like an empty Huntley & Palmer biscuit-tin kicked along a gutter; she was nothing so solid in make, and rather less pretty in shape, but I had expended enough hard work on her to make me love her. No influential friend would have served me better. She had given me a chance to come out a bit— to find out what I could do. No, I don't like work. I had rather laze about and think of all the fine things that can be done. I don't like work—no man does— but I like what is in the work—the chance to find yourself. Your own reality—for yourself, not for others—what no other man can ever know. They can only see the mere show, and never can tell what it really means.

"I was not surprised to see somebody sitting aft, on the deck, with his legs dangling over the mud. You see I rather chummed with the few mechanics there were in that station, whom the other pilgrims naturally despised—on account of their imperfect manners, I suppose. This was the foreman—a boiler-maker by trade—a good worker. He was a lank, bony, yellow-faced man, with big intense eyes. His aspect was worried, and his head was as bald as the palm of my hand; but his hair in falling seemed to have stuck to his chin, and had prospered in the new locality, for his beard hung down to his waist. He was a widower with six young children (he had left them in charge of a sister of his to come out there), and the passion of his life was pigeon-flying. He was an enthusiast and a connoisseur. He would rave about pigeons. After work hours he used sometimes to come over from his hut for a talk about his children and his pigeons; at work, when he had to crawl in the mud under the bottom of the steamboat, he would tie up that beard of his in a kind of white serviette he brought for the purpose. It had loops to go over his ears. In the evening he could be seen squatted on the bank rinsing that wrapper in the creek with great care, then spreading it solemnly on a bush to dry.

"I slapped him on the back and shouted, 'We shall have rivets!' He scrambled to his feet exclaiming, 'No! Rivets!' as though he couldn't believe his ears. Then in a low voice, 'You . . . eh?' I don't know why we behaved like lunatics. I put my finger to the side of my nose and nodded mysteriously. 'Good for you!' he cried, snapped his fingers above his head, lifting one foot. I tried a jig. We capered on the iron deck. A frightful clatter came out of that hulk, and the virgin forest on the other bank of the creek sent it back in a thundering roll upon the sleeping station. It must have made some of the pilgrims sit up in their hovels. A dark figure obscured the lighted doorway of the manager's hut, vanished, then, a second or so after, the doorway itself vanished, too. We stopped, and the silence driven away by the stamping of our feet flowed back again from the recesses of the land. The great wall of vegetation, an exuberant and entangled mass of trunks, branches, leaves, boughs, festoons, motionless in the moonlight, was like a rioting invasion of soundless life, a rolling wave of plants, piled up, crested, ready to topple over the creek, to sweep every little man of us out of his little existence. And it moved not. A deadened burst of mighty splashes and snorts reached us from afar, as though an ichthyo-

saurus had been taking a bath of glitter in the great
river. 'After all,' said the boiler-maker in a reasonable
tone, 'why shouldn't we get the rivets?' Why not, indeed! I did not know of any reason why we shouldn't.
'They'll come in three weeks,' I said confidently.

"But they didn't. Instead of rivets there came an
invasion, an infliction, a visitation. It came in sections
during the next three weeks, each section headed by
a donkey carrying a white man in new clothes and tan
shoes, bowing from that elevation right and left to the
impressed pilgrims. A quarrelsome band of footsore
sulky niggers trod on the heels of the donkey; a lot
of tents, campstools, tin boxes, white cases, brown
bales would be shot down in the court-yard, and the
air of mystery would deepen a little over the muddle
of the station. Five such instalments came, with their
absurd air of disorderly flight with the loot of innumerable outfit shops and provision stores, that, one
would think, they were lugging, after a raid, into the
wilderness for equitable division. It was an inextricable
mess of things decent in themselves but that human
folly made look like the spoils of thieving.

"This devoted band called itself the Eldorado Exploring Expedition, and I believe they were sworn to
secrecy. Their talk, however, was the talk of sordid
buccaneers: it was reckless without hardihood, greedy
without audacity, and cruel without courage; there was
not an atom of foresight or of serious intention in the
whole batch of them, and they did not seem aware
these things are wanted for the work of the world. To
tear treasure out of the bowels of the land was their
desire, with no more moral purpose at the back of it
than there is in burglars breaking into a safe. Who
paid the expenses of the noble enterprise I don't
know; but the uncle of our manager was leader of
that lot.

"In exterior he resembled a butcher in a poor neigh-
bourhood, and his eyes had a look of sleepy cunning.
He carried his fat paunch with ostentation on his short
legs, and during the time his gang infested the station

spoke to no one but his nephew. You could see these
two roaming about all day long with their heads close
together in an everlasting confab.

"I had given up worrying myself about the rivets.
One's capacity for that kind of folly is more limited
than you would suppose. I said Hang!—and let things
slide. I would give some thought to Kurtz. I wasn't
very interested in him. No. Still, I was curious to see
whether this man, who had come out equipped with
moral ideas of some sort, would climb to the top after
all and how he would set about his work when there."

II

"One evening as I was lying flat on the deck of my
steamboat, I heard voices approaching—and there
were the nephew and the uncle strolling along the
bank. I laid my head on my arm again, and had nearly
lost myself in a doze, when somebody said in my ear,
as it were: 'I am as harmless as a little child, but I
don't like to be dictated to. Am I the manager—or
am I not? I was ordered to send him there. It's
incredible.'. . . I became aware that the two were
standing on the shore alongside the forepart of the
steamboat, just below my head. I did not move; it did
not occur to me to move: I was sleepy. 'It *is* unpleasant,' grunted the uncle. 'He has asked the Administration to be sent there,' said the other, 'with the idea
of showing what he could do; and I was instructed
accordingly. Look at the influence that man must
have. Is it not frightful?' They both agreed it was
frightful, then made several bizarre remarks: 'Make
rain and fine weather—one man—the Council—by the
nose'—bits of absurd sentences that got the better of
my drowsiness, so that I had pretty near the whole of
my wits about me when the uncle said, 'The climate
may do away with this difficulty for you. Is he alone
there?' 'Yes,' answered the manager; 'he sent his assis-
tant down the river with a note to me in these terms:

"Clear this poor devil out of the country, and don't
bother sending more of that sort. I had rather be alone
than have the kind of men you can dispose of with
me." It was more than a year ago. Can you imagine
such impudence!' 'Anything since then?' asked the
other hoarsely. 'Ivory,' jerked the nephew; 'lots of it—
prime sort—lots—most annoying, from him.' 'And
with that?' questioned the heavy rumble. 'Invoice,'
was the reply fired out, so to speak. Then silence.
They had been talking about Kurtz.

    "I was broad awake by this time, but, lying perfectly
at ease, remained still, having no inducement to
change my position. 'How did that ivory come all this
way?' growled the elder man, who seemed very vexed.
The other explained that it had come with a fleet of
canoes in charge of an English half-caste clerk Kurtz
had with him; that Kurtz had apparently intended to
return himself, the station being by that time bare of
goods and stores, but after coming three hundred
miles, had suddenly decided to go back, which he
started to do alone in a small dugout with four pad-
dlers, leaving the half-caste to continue down the river
with the ivory. The two fellows there seemed astounded
at anybody attempting such a thing. They were at a
loss for an adequate motive. As to me, I seemed to
see Kurtz for the first time. It was a distant glimpse:
the dugout, four paddling savages, and the lone white
man turning his back suddenly on the headquarters,
on relief, on thoughts of home—perhaps; setting his
face towards the depths of the wilderness, towards his
empty and desolate station. I did not know the motive.
Perhaps he was just simply a fine fellow who stuck to
his work for its own sake. His name, you understand,
had not been pronounced once. He was 'that man.'
The half-caste, who, as far as I could see, had con-
ducted a difficult trip with great prudence and pluck,
was invariably alluded to as 'that scoundrel.' The
'scoundrel' had reported that the 'man' had been very
ill—had recovered imperfectly. . . . The two below me
moved away then a few paces, and strolled back and

forth at some little distance. I heard: 'Military post—
doctor—two hundred miles—quite alone now—
unavoidable delays—nine months—no news—strange
rumours.' They approached again, just as the manager
was saying, 'No one, as far as I know, unless a species
of wandering trader—a pestilential fellow, snapping
ivory from the natives.' Who was it they were talking
about now? I gathered in snatches that this was some
man supposed to be in Kurtz's district, and of whom
the manager did not approve. 'We will not be free
from unfair competition till one of these fellows is
hanged for an example,' he said. 'Certainly,' grunted
the other; 'get him hanged! Why not? Anything—
anything can be done in this country. That's what I
say; nobody here, you understand, *here,* can endanger
your position. And why? You stand the climate—you
outlast them all. The danger is in Europe; but there
before I left I took care to——' They moved off and
whispered, then their voices rose again. 'The extraordinary series of delays is not my fault. I did my best.'
The fat man sighed. 'Very sad.' 'And the pestiferous
absurdity of his talk,' continued the other; 'he bothered me enough when he was here. "Each station
should be like a beacon on the road towards better
things, a centre for trade of course, but also for hu-
manizing, improving, instructing." Conceive you—that
ass! And he wants to be manager! No, it's——' Here
he got choked by excessive indignation, and I lifted
my head the least bit. I was surprised to see how near
they were—right under me. I could have spat upon
their hats. They were looking on the ground, absorbed
in thought. The manager was switching his leg with a
slender twig: his sagacious relative lifted his head.
'You have been well since you came out this time?'
he asked. The other gave a start. 'Who? I? Oh! Like
a charm—like a charm. But the rest—oh, my goodness! All sick. They die so quick, too, that I haven't
the time to send them out of the country—it's incredible!' 'H'm. Just so,' grunted the uncle. 'Ah! my boy,
trust to this—I say, trust to this.' I saw him extend his

short flipper of an arm for a gesture that took in the
forest, the creek, the mud, the river—seemed to
beckon with a dishonouring flourish before the sunlit
face of the land a treacherous appeal to the lurking
death, to the hidden evil, to the profound darkness of
its heart. It was so startling that I leaped to my feet
and looked back at the edge of the forest, as though
I had expected an answer of some sort to that black
display of confidence. You know the foolish notions
that come to one sometimes. The high stillness confronted these two figures with its ominous patience,
waiting for the passing away of a fantastic invasion.

"They swore aloud together—out of sheer fright, I
believe—then pretending not to know anything of my
existence, turned back to the station. The sun was low;
and leaning forward side by side, they seemed to be
tugging painfully uphill their two ridiculous shadows
of unequal length, that trailed behind them slowly
over the tall grass without bending a single blade.

"In a few days the Eldorado Expedition went into
the patient wilderness, that closed upon it as the sea
closes over a diver. Long afterwards the news came
that all the donkeys were dead. I know nothing as to
the fate of the less valuable animals. They, no doubt,
like the rest of us, found what they deserved. I did
not inquire. I was then rather excited at the prospect
of meeting Kurtz very soon. When I say very soon I
mean it comparatively. It was just two months from
the day we left the creek when we came to the bank
below Kurtz's station.

"Going up that river was like travelling back to the
earliest beginnings of the world, when vegetation rioted on the earth and the big trees were kings. An
empty stream, a great silence, an impenetrable forest.
The air was warm, thick, heavy, sluggish. There was
no joy in the brilliance of sunshine. The long stretches
of the waterway ran on, deserted, into the gloom of
over-shadowed distances. On silvery sand-banks hippos
and alligators sunned themselves side by side. The
broadening waters flowed through a mob of wooded

islands; you lost your way on that river as you would
in a desert, and butted all day long against shoals,
trying to find the channel, till you thought yourself
bewitched and cut off for ever from everything you
had known once—somewhere—far away—in another
existence perhaps. There were moments when one's
past came back to one, as it will sometimes when you
have not a moment to spare to yourself; but it came
in the shape of an unrestful and noisy dream, remembered with wonder amongst the overwhelming realities of this strange world of plants, and water, and
silence. And this stillness of life did not in the least
resemble a peace. It was the stillness of an implacable
force brooding over an inscrutable intention. It looked
at you with a vengeful aspect. I got used to it afterwards; I did not see it any more; I had no time. I had
to keep guessing at the channel; I had to discern,
mostly by inspiration, the signs of hidden banks; I
watched for sunken stones; I was learning to clap my
teeth smartly before my heart flew out, when I shaved
by a fluke some infernal sly old snag that would have
ripped the life out of the tin-pot steamboat and
drowned all the pilgrims; I had to keep a lookout for
the signs of dead wood we could cut up in the night
for next day's steaming. When you have to attend to
things of that sort, to the mere incidents of the surface,
the reality—the reality, I tell you—fades. The inner
truth is hidden—luckily, luckily. But I felt it all the
same; I felt often its mysterious stillness watching me
at my monkey tricks, just as it watches you fellows
performing on your respective tight-ropes for—what
is it? half-a-crown a tumble——"

"Try to be civil, Marlow," growled a voice, and I
knew there was at least one listener awake besides
myself.

"I beg your pardon. I forgot the heartache which
makes up the rest of the price. And indeed what does
the price matter, if the trick be well done? You do
your tricks very well. And I didn't do badly either,
since I managed not to sink that steamboat on my first

trip. It's a wonder to me yet. Imagine a blindfolded
man set to drive a van over a bad road. I sweated and
shivered over that business considerably, I can tell
you. After all, for a seaman, to scrape the bottom of
the thing that's supposed to float all the time under
his care is the unpardonable sin. No one may know
of it, but you never forget the thump—eh? A blow on
the very heart. You remember it, you dream of it, you
wake up at night and think of it—years after—and go
hot and cold all over. I don't pretend to say that
steamboat floated all the time. More than once she
had to wade for a bit, with twenty cannibals splashing
around and pushing. We had enlisted some of these
chaps on the way for a crew. Fine fellows—cannibals—
in their place. They were men one could work with,
and I am grateful to them. And, after all, they did not
eat each other before my face: they had brought along
a provision of hippo-meat which went rotten, and
made the mystery of the wilderness stink in my nostrils. Phoo! I can sniff it now. I had the manager on
board and three or four pilgrims with their staves—
all complete. Sometimes we came upon a station close
by the bank, clinging to the skirts of the unknown,
and the white men rushing out of a tumble-down
hovel, with great gestures of joy and surprise and welcome, seemed very strange—had the appearance of
being held there captive by a spell. The word ivory
would ring in the air for a while—and on we went
again into the silence, along empty reaches, round the
still bends, between the high walls of our winding way,
reverberating in hollow claps the ponderous beat of
the stern-wheel. Trees, trees, millions of trees, mas-
sive, immense, running up high; and at their foot, hug-
ging the bank against the stream, crept the little
begrimed steamboat, like a sluggish beetle crawling on
the floor of a lofty portico. It made you feel very
small, very lost, and yet it was not altogether de-
pressing, that feeling. After all, if you were small, the
grimy beetle crawled on—which was just what you
wanted it to do. Where the pilgrims imagined it crawled

to I don't know. To some place where they expected
to get something, I bet! For me it crawled towards
Kurtz—exclusively; but when the steam-pipes started
leaking we crawled very slow. The reaches opened
before us and closed behind, as if the forest had
stepped leisurely across the water to bar the way for
our return. We penetrated deeper and deeper into the
heart of darkness. It was very quiet there. At night
sometimes the roll of drums behind the curtain of
trees would run up the river and remain sustained
faintly, as if hovering in the air high over our heads,
till the first break of day. Whether it meant war, peace,
or prayer we could not tell. The dawns were heralded
by the descent of a chill stillness; the wood-cutters
slept, their fires burned low; the snapping of a twig
would make you start. We were wanderers on a prehistoric earth, on an earth that wore the aspect of an
unknown planet. We could have fancied ourselves the
first of men taking possession of an accursed inheritance, to be subdued at the cost of profound anguish
and of excessive toil. But suddenly, as we struggled
round a bend, there would be a glimpse of rush walls,
of peaked grass-roofs, a burst of yells, a whirl of black
limbs, a mass of hands clapping, of feet stamping, of
bodies swaying, of eyes rolling, under the droop of
heavy and motionless foliage. The steamer toiled
along slowly on the edge of a black and incomprehensible frenzy. The prehistoric man was cursing us, praying to us, welcoming us—who could tell? We were cut
off from the comprehension of our surroundings; we
glided past like phantoms, wondering and secretly appalled, as sane men would be before an enthusiastic
outbreak in a madhouse. We could not understand
because we were too far and could not remember because we were travelling in the night of first ages, of
those ages that are gone, leaving hardly a sign—and
no memories.

"The earth seemed unearthly. We are accustomed
to look upon the shackled form of a conquered monster,
but there—there you could look at a thing monstrous

and free. It was unearthly, and the men were—— No,
they were not inhuman. Well, you know, that was the
worst of it—this suspicion of their not being inhuman.
It would come slowly to one. They howled and leaped,
and spun, and made horrid faces; but what thrilled
you was just the thought of their humanity—like
yours—the thought of your remote kinship with this
wild and passionate uproar. Ugly. Yes, it was ugly
enough; but if you were man enough you would admit
to yourself that there was in you just the faintest trace
of a response to the terrible frankness of that noise,
a dim suspicion of there being a meaning in it which
you—you so remote from the night of first ages—
could comprehend. And why not? The mind of man
is capable of anything—because everything is in it, all
the past as well as all the future. What was there after
all? Joy, fear, sorrow, devotion, valour, rage—who can
tell?—but truth—truth stripped of its cloak of time.
Let the fool gape and shudder—the man knows, and
can look on without a wink. But he must at least be
as much of a man as these on the shore. He must meet
the truth with his own true stuff—with his own inborn
strength. Principles won't do. Acquisitions, clothes,
pretty rags—rags that would fly off at the first good
shake. No; you want a deliberate belief. An appeal to
me in this fiendish row—is there? Very well; I hear; I
admit, but I have a voice, too, and for good or evil
mine is the speech that cannot be silenced. Of course,
a fool, what with sheer fright and fine sentiments, is
always safe. Who's that grunting? You wonder I didn't
go ashore for a howl and a dance? Well, no—I didn't.
Fine sentiments, you say? Fine sentiments, be hanged!
I had no time. I had to mess about with white-lead
and strips of woolen blanket helping to put bandages
on those leaky steam-pipes—I tell you. I had to watch
the steering, and circumvent those snags, and get the
tin-pot along by hook or by crook. There was surface-
truth enough in these things to save a wiser man. And
between whiles I had to look after the savage who
was fireman. He was an improved specimen; he could

fire up a vertical boiler. He was there below me, and, upon my word, to look at him was as edifying as seeing a dog in a parody of breeches and a feather hat, walking on his hind-legs. A few months of training had done for that really fine chap. He squinted at the steam-gauge and at the water-gauge with an evident effort of intrepidity—and he had filed teeth, too, the poor devil, and the wool of his pate shaved into queer patterns, and three ornamental scars on each of his cheeks. He ought to have been clapping his hands and stamping his feet on the bank, instead of which he was hard at work, a thrall to strange witchcraft, full of improving knowledge. He was useful because he had been instructed; and what he knew was this—that should the water in that transparent thing disappear, the evil spirit inside the boiler would get angry through the greatness of his thirst, and take a terrible vengeance. So he sweated and fired up and watched the glass fearfully (with an impromptu charm, made of rags, tied to his arm, and a piece of polished bone, as big as a watch, stuck flatways through his lower lip), while the wooded banks slipped past us slowly, the short noise was left behind, the interminable miles of silence—and we crept on, towards Kurtz. But the snags were thick, the water was treacherous and shallow, the boiler seemed indeed to have a sulky devil in it, and thus neither that fireman nor I had any time to peer into our creepy thoughts.

"Some fifty miles below the Inner Station we came upon a hut of reeds, an inclined and melancholy pole, with the unrecognizable tatters of what had been a flag of some sort flying from it, and a neatly stacked wood-pile. This was unexpected. We came to the bank, and on the stack of firewood found a flat piece of board with some faded pencil-writing on it. When deciphered it said: 'Wood for you. Hurry up. Approach cautiously.' There was a signature, but it was illegible—not Kurtz—a much longer word. 'Hurry up.' Where? Up the river? 'Approach cautiously.' We had not done so. But the warning could not have been

meant for the place where it could be only found after
approach. Something was wrong above. But what—and
how much? That was the question. We commented ad-
versely upon the imbecility of that telegraphic style. The
bush around said nothing, and would not let us look
very far, either. A torn curtain of red twill hung in
the doorway of the hut, and flapped sadly in our faces.
The dwelling was dismantled; but we could see a white
man had lived there not very long ago. There remained a rude table—a plank of two posts; a heap of
rubbish reposed in a dark corner, and by the door I
picked up a book. It had lost its covers, and the pages
had been thumbed into a state of extremely dirty soft-
ness; but the back had been lovingly stitched afresh
with white cotton thread, which looked clean yet. It
was an extraordinary find. Its title was, *An Inquiry
into Some Points of Seamanship,* by a man Towser,
Towson—some such name—Master in his Majesty's
Navy. The matter looked dreary reading enough, with
illustrative diagrams and repulsive tables of figures,
and the copy was sixty years old. I handled this amazing antiquity with the greatest possible tenderness, lest
it should dissolve in my hands. Within, Towson or
Towser was inquiring earnestly into the breaking
strain of ships' chains and tackles, and other such matters. Not a very enthralling book; but at the first
glance you could see there a singleness of intention,
an honest concern for the right way of going to work,
which made these humble pages, thought out so many
years ago, luminous with another than a professional
light. The simple old sailor, with his talk of chains and
purchases, made me forget the jungle and the pilgrims
in a delicious sensation of having come upon something unmistakably real. Such a book being there was
wonderful enough; but still more astounding were the
notes pencilled in the margin, and plainly referring to
the text. I couldn't believe my eyes! They were in
cipher! Yes, it looked like cipher. Fancy a man lugging
with him a book of that description into this nowhere

and studying it—and making notes—in cipher at that! It was an extravagant mystery.

"I had been dimly aware for some time of a worrying noise, and when I lifted my eyes I saw the wood-pile was gone, and the manager, aided by all the pilgrims, was shouting at me from the riverside. I slipped the book into my pocket. I assure you to leave off reading was like tearing myself away from the shelter of an old and solid friendship.

"I started the lame engine ahead. 'It must be this miserable trader—this intruder,' exclaimed the manager, looking back malevolently at the place we had left. 'He must be English,' I said. 'It will not save him from getting into trouble if he is not careful,' muttered the manager darkly. I observed with assumed innocence that no man was safe from trouble in this world.

"The current was more rapid now, the steamer seemed at her last gasp, the stern-wheel flopped languidly, and I caught myself listening on tiptoe for the next beat of the boat, for in sober truth I expected the wretched thing to give up every moment. It was like watching the last flickers of a life. But still we crawled. Sometimes I would pick out a tree a little way ahead to measure our progress towards Kurtz by, but I lost it invariably before we got abreast. To keep the eyes so long on one thing was too much for human patience. The manager displayed a beautiful resignation. I fretted and fumed and took to arguing with myself whether or no I would talk openly with Kurtz; but before I could come to any conclusion it occurred to me that my speech or my silence, indeed any action of mine, would be a mere futility. What did it matter what any one knew or ignored? What did it matter who was manager? One gets sometimes such a flash of insight. The essentials of this affair lay deep under the surface, beyond my reach, and beyond my power of meddling.

"Towards the evening of the second day we judged ourselves about eight miles from Kurtz's station. I

wanted to push on; but the manager looked grave,
and told me the navigation up there was so dangerous
that it would be advisable, the sun being very low
already, to wait where we were till next morning.
Moreover, he pointed out that if the warning to approach cautiously were to be followed, we must approach in daylight—not at dusk or in the dark. This
was sensible enough. Eight miles meant nearly three
hours' steaming for us, and I could also see suspicious
ripples at the upper end of the reach. Nevertheless, I
was annoyed beyond expression at the delay, and most
unreasonably, too, since one night more could not
matter much after so many months. As we had plenty
of wood, and caution was the word, I brought up in
the middle of the stream. The reach was narrow,
straight, with high sides like a railway cutting. The
dusk came gliding into it long before the sun had set.
The current ran smooth and swift, but a dumb immobility sat on the banks. The living trees, lashed together by the creepers and every living bush of the
undergrowth, might have been changed into stone,
even to the slenderest twig, to the lightest leaf. It was
not sleep—it seemed unnatural, like a state of trance.
Not the faintest sound of any kind could be heard.
You looked on amazed, and began to suspect yourself
of being deaf—then the night came suddenly, and
struck you blind as well. About three in the morning
some large fish leaped, and the loud splash made me
jump as though a gun had been fired. When the sun
rose there was a white fog, very warm and clammy,
and more blinding than the night. It did not shift or
drive; it was just there, standing all round you like
something solid. At eight or nine, perhaps, it lifted as
a shutter lifts. We had a glimpse of the towering multitude of trees, of the immense matted jungle, with the
blazing little ball of the sun hanging over it—all perfectly still—and then the white shutter came down
again, smoothly, as if sliding in greased grooves. I ordered the chain, which we had begun to heave in, to
be paid out again. Before it stopped running with a

muffled rattle, a cry, a very loud cry, as of infinite desolation, soared slowly in the opaque air. It ceased. A complaining clamour, modulated in savage discords, filled our ears. The sheer unexpectedness of it made my hair stir under my cap. I don't know how it struck the others: to me it seemed as though the mist itself had screamed, so suddenly, and apparently from all sides at once, did this tumultuous and mournful uproar arise. It culminated in a hurried outbreak of almost intolerably excessive shrieking, which stopped short, leaving us stiffened in a variety of silly attitudes, and obstinately listening to the nearly as appalling and excessive silence. 'Good God! What is the meaning——' stammered at my elbow one of the pilgrims—a little fat man, with sandy hair and red whiskers, who wore sidespring boots, and pink pyjamas tucked into his socks. Two others remained open-mouthed a whole minute, then dashed into the little cabin, to rush out incontinently and stand darting scared glances, with Winchesters at 'ready' in their hands. What we could see was just the steamer we were on, her outlines blurred as though she had been on the point of dissolving, and a misty strip of water, perhaps two feet broad, around her—and that was all. The rest of the world was nowhere, as far as our eyes and ears were concerned. Just nowhere. Gone, disappeared; swept off without leaving a whisper or a shadow behind.

"I went forward, and ordered the chain to be hauled in short, so as to be ready to trip the anchor and move the steamboat at once if necessary. 'Will they attack?' whispered an awed voice. 'We will be all butchered in this fog,' murmured another. The faces twitched with the strain, the hands trembled slightly, the eyes forgot to wink. It was very curious to see the contrast of expressions of the white men and of the black fellows of our crew, who were as much strangers to that part of the river as we, though their homes were only eight hundred miles away. The whites, of course greatly discomposed, had besides a curious look of being painfully shocked by such an outrageous row. The others

had an alert, naturally interested expression; but their
faces were essentially quiet, even those of the one or
two who grinned as they hauled at the chain. Several
exchanged short, grunting phrases, which seemed to
settle the matter to their satisfaction. Their headman,
a young, broad-chested black, severely draped in dark-
blue fringed cloths, with fierce nostrils and his hair all
done up artfully in oily ringlets, stood near me. 'Aha!'
I said, just for good fellowship's sake. 'Catch 'im,' he
snapped, with a bloodshot widening of his eyes and a
flash of sharp teeth—'catch 'im. Give 'im to us.' 'To
you, eh?' I asked; 'what would you do with them?'
'Eat 'im!' he said curtly, and, leaning his elbow on the
rail, looked out into the fog in a dignified and profoundly pensive attitude. I would no doubt have been
properly horrified, had it not occurred to me that he
and his chaps must be very hungry: that they must
have been growing increasingly hungry for at least this
month past. They had been engaged for six months (I
don't think a single one of them had any clear idea
of time, as we at the end of countless ages have. They
still belonged to the beginnings of time—had no inher-
ited experience to teach them as it were), and of
course, as long as there was a piece of paper written
over in accordance with some farcical law or other
made down the river, it didn't enter anybody's head
to trouble how they would live. Certainly they had
brought with them some rotten hippo-meat, which
couldn't have lasted very long, anyway, even if the
pilgrims hadn't, in the midst of a shocking hullabaloo,
thrown a considerable quantity of it overboard. It
looked like a high-handed proceeding; but it was really
a case of legitimate self-defence. You can't breathe
dead hippo waking, sleeping, and eating, and at the
same time keep your precarious grip on existence. Besides that, they had given them every week three
pieces of brass wire, each about nine inches long; and
the theory was they were to buy their provisions with
that currency in riverside villages. You can see how
that worked. There were either no villages, or the peo-

ple were hostile, or the director, who like the rest of
us fed out of tins, with an occasional old he-goat
thrown in, didn't want to stop the steamer for some
more or less recondite reason. So, unless they swallowed the wire itself, or made loops of it to snare the
fishes with, I don't see what good their extravagant
salary could do to them. I must say it was paid with
a regularity worthy of a large and honourable trading
company. For the rest, the only thing to eat—though
it didn't look eatable in the least—I saw in their possession was a few lumps of some stuff like half-cooked
dough, of a dirty lavender colour, they kept wrapped
in leaves, and now and then swallowed a piece of, but
so small that it seemed done more for the looks of
the thing than for any serious purpose of sustenance.
Why in the name of all the gnawing devils of hunger
they didn't go for us—they were thirty to five—and
have a good tuck-in for once, amazes me now when I
think of it. They were big powerful men, with not
much capacity to weigh the consequences, with courage, with strength, even yet, though their skins were
no longer glossy and their muscles no longer hard.
And I saw that something restraining, one of those
human secrets that baffle probability, had come into
play there. I looked at them with a swift quickening
of interest—not because it occurred to me I might be
eaten by them before very long, though I own to you
that just then I perceived—in a new light, as it were—
how unwholesome the pilgrims looked, and I hoped,
yes, I positively hoped, that my aspect was not so—
what shall I say?—so—unappetizing: a touch of fantastic vanity which fitted well with the dream-sensation
that pervaded all my days at that time. Perhaps I had
a little fever, too. One can't live with one's finger ever-
lastingly on one's pulse. I had often 'a little fever,' or
a little touch of other things—the playful paw-strokes
of the wilderness, the preliminary trifling before the
more serious onslaught which came in due course.
Yes; I looked at them as you would on any human
being, with a curiosity of their impulses, motives, ca-

pacities, weaknesses, when brought to the test of an
inexorable physical necessity. Restraint! What possible
restraint? Was it superstition, disgust, patience, fear—
or some kind of primitive honour? No fear can stand
up to hunger, no patience can wear it out, disgust
simply does not exist where hunger is; and as to superstition, beliefs, and what you may call principles, they
are less than chaff in a breeze. Don't you know the
devilry of lingering starvation, its exasperating torment, its black thoughts, its sombre and brooding ferocity? Well, I do. It takes a man all his inborn
strength to fight hunger properly. It's really easier to
face bereavement, dishonour, and the perdition of
one's soul—than this kind of prolonged hunger. Sad,
but true. And these chaps, too, had no earthly reason
for any kind of scruple. Restraint! I would just as soon
have expected restraint from a hyena prowling
amongst the corpses of a battlefield. But there was the
fact facing me—the fact dazzling, to be seen, like the
foam on the depths of the sea, like a ripple on an
unfathomable enigma, a mystery greater—when I
thought of it—than the curious, inexplicable note of
desperate grief in this savage clamour that had swept
by us on the river-bank, behind the blind whiteness
of the fog.

"Two pilgrims were quarrelling in hurried whispers
as to which bank. 'Left.' 'No, no; how can you? Right,
right, of course.' 'It is very serious,' said the manager's
voice behind me; 'I would be desolated if anything
should happen to Mr. Kurtz before we came up.' I
looked at him, and had not the slightest doubt he was
sincere. He was just the kind of man who would wish
to preserve appearances. That was his restraint. But
when he muttered something about going on at once,
I did not even take the trouble to answer him. I knew,
and he knew, that it was impossible. Were we to let
go our hold of the bottom, we would be absolutely in
the air—in space. We wouldn't be able to tell where
we were going to—whether up or down stream, or
across—till we fetched against one bank or the

other—and then we wouldn't know at first which it was. Of course I made no move. I had no mind for a smash-up. You couldn't imagine a more deadly place for a shipwreck. Whether drowned at once or not, we were sure to perish speedily in one way or another. 'I authorize you to take all the risks,' he said, after a short silence. 'I refuse to take any,' I said shortly; which was just the answer he expected, though its tone might have surprised him. 'Well, I must defer to your judgment. You are captain,' he said with marked civility. I turned my shoulder to him in sign of my appreciation, and looked into the fog. How long would it last? It was the most hopeless lookout. The approach to this Kurtz grubbing for ivory in the wretched bush was beset by as many dangers as though he had been an enchanted princess sleeping in a fabulous castle. "Will they attack, do you think?" asked the manager, in a confidential tone.

"I did not think they would attack, for several obvious reasons. The thick fog was one. If they left the bank in their canoes they would get lost in it, as we would be if we attempted to move. Still, I had also judged the jungle of both banks quite impenetrable— and yet eyes were in it, eyes that had seen us. The riverside bushes were certainly very thick; but the undergrowth behind was evidently penetrable. However, during the short lift I had seen no canoes anywhere in the reach—certainly not abreast of the steamer. But what made the idea of attack inconceivable to me was the nature of the noise—of the cries we had heard. They had not the fierce character boding immediate hostile intention. Unexpected, wild, and violent as they had been, they had given me an irresistible impression of sorrow. The glimpse of the steamboat had for some reason filled those savages with unrestrained grief. The danger, if any, I expounded, was from our proximity to a great human passion let loose. Even extreme grief may ultimately vent itself in violence— but more generally takes the form of apathy. . . .

"You should have seen the pilgrims stare! They had

no heart to grin, or even to revile me: but I believe
they thought me gone mad—with fright, maybe. I de-
livered a regular lecture. My dear boys, it was no good
bothering. Keep a lookout? Well, you may guess I
watched the fog for the signs of lifting as a cat watches
a mouse; but for anything else were of no more use
to us than if we had been buried miles deep in a heap
of cotton-wool. It felt like it, too—choking, warm, sti-
fling. Besides, all I said, though it sounded extravagant, was absolutely true to fact. What we afterwards
alluded to as an attack was really an attempt to re-
pulse. The action was very far from being aggressive—
it was not even defensive, in the usual sense: it was
undertaken under the stress of desperation, and in its
essence was purely protective.

"It developed itself, I should say, two hours after
the fog lifted, and its commencement was at a spot,
roughly speaking, about a mile and a half below
Kurtz's station. We had just floundered and flopped
round a bend, when I saw an islet, a mere grassy hum-
mock of bright green, in the middle of the stream. It
was the only thing of the kind; but as we opened the
reach more, I perceived it was the head of a long
sand-bank, or rather of a chain of shallow patches
stretching down the middle of the river. They were
discoloured, just awash, and the whole lot was seen
just under the water, exactly as a man's backbone is
seen running down the middle of his back under the
skin. Now, as far as I did see, I could go to the right
or to the left of this. I didn't know either channel, of
course. The banks looked pretty well alike, the depth
appeared the same; but as I had been informed the
station was on the west side, I naturally headed for
the western passage.

"No sooner had we fairly entered it than I became
aware it was much narrower than I had supposed. To
the left of us there was the long uninterrupted shoal,
and to the right a high, steep bank heavily overgrown
with bushes. Above the bush the trees stood in serried
ranks. The twigs overhung the current thickly, and

from distance to distance a large limb of some tree
projected rigidly over the stream. It was then well on
in the afternoon, the face of the forest was gloomy,
and a broad strip of shadow had already fallen on the
water. In this shadow we steamed up—very slowly, as
you may imagine. I sheered her well inshore—the
water being deepest near the bank, as the sounding-
pole informed me.

"One of my hungry and forbearing friends was
sounding in the bows just below me. This steamboat
was exactly like a decked scow. On the deck, there
were two little teakwood houses, with doors and windows. The boiler was in the fore-end, and the machinery right astern. Over the whole there was a light roof,
supported on stanchions. The funnel projected through
that roof, and in front of the funnel a small cabin built
of light planks served for a pilot-house. It contained
a couch, two camp-stools, a loaded Martini-Henry
leaning in one corner, a tiny table, and the steering-
wheel. It had a wide door in front and a broad shutter
at each side. All these were always thrown open, of
course. I spent my days perched up there on the extreme fore-end of that roof, before the door. At night
I slept, or tried to, on the couch. An athletic black
belonging to some coast tribe, and educated by my
poor predecessor, was the helmsman. He sported a
pair of brass earrings, wore a blue cloth wrapper from
the waist to the ankles, and thought all the world of
himself. He was the most unstable kind of fool I had
ever seen. He steered with no end of a swagger while
you were by; but if he lost sight of you, he became
instantly the prey of an abject funk, and would let that
cripple of a steamboat get the upper hand of him in
a minute.

"I was looking down at the sounding-pole, and feeling much annoyed to see at each try a little more of
it stick out of that river, when I saw my poleman give
up the business suddenly, and stretch himself flat on
the deck, without even taking the trouble to haul his
pole in. He kept hold on it though, and it trailed in

the water. At the same time the fireman, whom I
could also see below me, sat down abruptly before his
furnace and ducked his head. I was amazed. Then I
had to look at the river mighty quick, because there
was a snag in the fairway. Sticks, little sticks, were
flying about—thick: they were whizzing before my
nose, dropping below me, striking behind me against
my pilot-house. All this time the river, the shore, the
woods, were very quiet—perfectly quiet. I could only
hear the heavy splashing thump of the stern-wheel and
the patter of these things. We cleared the snag clum-
sily. Arrows, by Jove! We were being shot at! I
stepped in quickly to close the shutter on the landside.
That fool-helmsman, his hands on the spokes, was lifting his knees high, stamping his feet, champing his
mouth, like a reined-in horse. Confound him! And we
were staggering within ten feet of the bank. I had to
lean right out to swing the heavy shutter, and I saw a
face amongst the leaves on the level with my own,
looking at me very fierce and steady; and then suddenly, as though a veil had been removed from my
eyes, I made out, deep in the tangled gloom, naked
breasts, arms, legs, glaring eyes—the bush was swarm-
ing with human limbs in movement, glistening, of
bronze colour. The twigs shook, swayed, and rustled,
the arrows flew out of them, and then the shutter came
to. 'Steer her straight,' I said to the helmsman. He
held his head rigid, face forward; but his eyes rolled,
he kept on lifting and setting down his feet gently, his
mouth foamed a little. 'Keep quiet!' I said in a fury.
I might just as well have ordered a tree not to sway
in the wind. I darted out. Below me there was a great
scuffle of feet on the iron deck; confused exclamations;
a voice screamed, 'Can you turn back?' I caught sight
of a V-shaped ripple on the water ahead. What? Another snag? A fusillade burst out under my feet. The
pilgrims had opened with their Winchesters, and were
simply squirting lead into that bush. A deuce of a lot
of smoke came up and drove slowly forward. I swore
at it. Now I couldn't see the ripple or the snag either.

I stood in the doorway, peering, and the arrows came in swarms. They might have been poisoned, but they looked as though they wouldn't kill a cat. The bush began to howl. Our wood-cutters raised a warlike whoop; the report of a rifle just at my back deafened me. I glanced over my shoulder, and the pilot-house was yet full of noise and smoke when I made a dash at the wheel. The fool-nigger had dropped everything, to throw the shutter open and let off that Martini-Henry. He stood before the wide opening, glaring, and I yelled at him to come back, while I straightened the sudden twist out of that steamboat. There was no room to turn even if I had wanted to, the snag was somewhere very near ahead in that confounded smoke, there was no time to lose, so I just crowded her into the bank—right into the bank, where I knew the water was deep.

"We tore slowly along the overhanging bushes in a whirl of broken twigs and flying leaves. The fusillade below stopped short, as I had foreseen it would when the squirts got empty. I threw my head back to a glinting whizz that traversed the pilot-house, in at one shutter-hole and out at the other. Looking past that mad helmsman, who was shaking the empty rifle and yelling at the shore, I saw vague forms of men running bent double, leaping, gliding, distinct, incomplete, eva-nescent. Something big appeared in the air before the shutter, the rifle went overboard, and the man stepped back swiftly, looked at me over his shoulder in an extraordinary, profound, familiar manner, and fell upon my feet. The side of his head hit the wheel twice, and the end of what appeared a long cane clattered round and knocked over a little camp-stool. It looked as though after wrenching that thing from somebody ashore he had lost his balance in the effort. The thin smoke had blown away, we were clear of the snag, and looking ahead I could see that in another hundred yards or so I would be free to sheer off, away from the bank; but my feet felt so very warm and wet that I had to look down. The man had rolled on his back

and stared straight up at me; both his hands clutched
that cane. It was the shaft of a spear that, either
thrown or lunged through the opening, had caught
him in the side just below the ribs; the blade had gone
in out of sight, after making a frightful gash; my shoes
were full; a pool of blood lay very still, gleaming dark-
red under the wheel; his eyes shone with an amazing
lustre. The fusillade burst out again. He looked at me
anxiously, gripping the spear like something precious,
with an air of being afraid I would try to take it away
from him. I had to make an effort to free my eyes
from his gaze and attend to the steering. With one
hand I felt above my head for the line of the steam
whistle, and jerked out screech after screech hurriedly.
The tumult of angry and warlike yells was checked
instantly, and then from the depths of the woods went
out such a tremulous and prolonged wail of mournful
fear and utter despair as may be imagined to follow
the flight of the last hope from the earth. There was
a great commotion in the bush; the shower of arrows
stopped, a few dropping shots rang out sharply—then
silence, in which the languid beat of the stern-wheel
came plainly to my ears. I put the helm hard a-
starboard at the moment when the pilgrim in pink
pyjamas, very hot and agitated, appeared in the doorway. 'The manager sends me——' he began in an official tone, and stopped short. 'Good God!'' he said,
glaring at the wounded man.

"We two whites stood over him, and his lustrous
and inquiring glance enveloped us both. I declare it
looked as though he would presently put to us some
question in an understandable language; but he died
without uttering a sound, without moving a limb, without twitching a muscle. Only in the very last moment,
as though in response to some sign we could not see,
to some whisper we could not hear, he frowned heavily, and that frown gave to his black death-mask an
inconceivably sombre, brooding, and menacing expression. The lustre of inquiring glance faded swiftly into
vacant glassiness. 'Can you steer?' I asked the agent

eagerly. He looked very dubious; but I made a grab at his arm, and he understood at once I meant him to steer whether or no. To tell you the truth, I was morbidly anxious to change my shoes and socks. 'He is dead,' murmured the fellow, immensely impressed. 'No doubt about it,' said I, tugging like mad at the shoe-laces. 'And by the way, I suppose Mr. Kurtz is dead as well by this time.'

"For the moment that was the dominant thought. There was a sense of extreme disappointment, as though I had found out I had been striving after something altogether without a substance. I couldn't have been more disgusted if I had travelled all this way for the sole purpose of talking with Mr. Kurtz. Talking with . . . I flung one shoe overboard, and became aware that that was exactly what I had been looking forward to—a talk with Kurtz. I made the strange discovery that I had never imagined him as doing, you know, but as discoursing. I didn't say to myself, 'Now I will never see him,' or 'Now I will never shake him by the hand,' but, 'Now I will never hear him.' The man presented himself as a voice. Not of course that I did not connect him with some sort of action. Hadn't I been told in all the tones of jealousy and admiration that he had collected, bartered, swindled, or stolen more ivory than all the other agents together? That was not the point. The point was in his being a gifted creature, and that of all his gifts the one that stood out preëminently, that carried with it a sense of real presence, was his ability to talk, his words—the gift of expression, the bewildering, the illuminating, the most exalted and the most contemptible, the pulsating stream of light, or the deceitful flow from the heart of an impenetrable darkness.

"The other shoe went flying unto the devil-god of that river. I thought, 'By Jove! it's all over. We are too late; he has vanished—the gift has vanished, by means of some spear, arrow, or club. I will never hear that chap speak after all'—and my sorrow had a startling extravagance of emotion, even such as I had no-

ticed in the howling sorrow of these savages in the
bush. I couldn't have felt more of lonely desolation
somehow, had I been robbed of a belief or had missed my
destiny in life. . . . Why do you sigh in this beastly way,
somebody? Absurd? Well, absurd. Good Lord! mustn't
a man ever——— Here, give me some tobacco." . . .

There was a pause of profound stillness, then a
match flared, and Marlow's lean face appeared, worn,
hollow, with downward folds and dropped eyelids,
with an aspect of concentrated attention; and as he
took vigorous draws at his pipe, it seemed to retreat
and advance out of the night in the regular flicker of
tiny flame. The match went out.

"Absurd!" he cried. "This is the worst of trying to
tell. . . . Here you all are, each moored with two good
addresses, like a hulk with two anchors, a butcher
round one corner, a policeman round another, excellent appetites, and temperature normal—you hear—
normal from year's end to year's end. And you say,
Absurd! Absurd be—exploded! Absurd! My dear
boys, what can you expect from a man who out of
sheer nervousness had just flung overboard a pair of
new shoes! Now I think of it, it is amazing I did not
shed tears. I am, upon the whole, proud of my forti-
tude. I was cut to the quick at the idea of having lost
the inestimable privilege of listening to the gifted
Kurtz. Of course I was wrong. The privilege was waiting for me. Oh, yes, I heard more than enough. And
I was right, too. A voice. He was very little more
than a voice. And I heard—him—it—this voice—other
voices—all of them were so little more than voices—
and the memory of that time itself lingers around me,
impalpable, like a dying vibration of one immense jab-
ber, silly, atrocious, sordid, savage, or simply mean,
without any kind of sense. Voices, voices—even the
girl herself—now———"

He was silent for a long time.

"I laid the ghost of his gifts at last with a lie," he
began, suddenly. "Girl! What? Did I mention a girl?
Oh, she is out of it—completely. They—the women I

mean—are out of it—should be out of it. We must
help them to stay in that beautiful world of their own,
lest ours gets worse. Oh, she had to be out of it. You
should have heard the disinterred body of Mr. Kurtz
saying, 'My Intended.' You would have perceived directly then how completely she was out of it. And the
lofty frontal bone of Mr. Kurtz! They say the hair
goes on growing sometimes, but this—ah—specimen,
was impressively bald. The wilderness had patted him
on the head, and, behold, it was like a ball—an ivory
ball; it had caressed him, and—lo!—he had withered;
it had taken him, loved him, embraced him, got into
his veins, consumed his flesh, and sealed his soul to its
own by the inconceivable ceremonies of some devilish
initiation. He was its spoiled and pampered favourite.
Ivory? I should think so. Heaps of it, stacks of it. The
old mud shanty was bursting with it. You would think
there was not a single tusk left either above or below
the ground in the whole country. 'Mostly fossil,' the
manager had remarked, disparagingly. It was no more
fossil than I am; but they call it fossil when it is dug
up. It appears these niggers do bury the tusks
sometimes—but evidently they couldn't bury this par-
cel deep enough to save the gifted Mr. Kurtz from his
fate. We filled the steamboat with it, and had to pile
a lot on the deck. Thus he could see and enjoy as long
as he could see, because the appreciation of this favour had remained with him to the last. You should
have heard him say, 'My ivory.' Oh, yes, I heard him.
'My Intended, my ivory, my station, my river, my——'
everything belonged to him. It made me hold my
breath in expectation of hearing the wilderness burst
into a prodigious peal of laughter that would shake
the fixed stars in their places. Everything belonged to
him—but that was a trifle. The thing was to know
what he belonged to, how many powers of darkness
claimed him for their own. That was the reflection that
made you creepy all over. It was impossible—it was
not good for one either—trying to imagine. He had
taken a high seat amongst the devils of the land—I

mean literally. You can't understand. How could
you?—with solid pavement under your feet, surrounded by kind neighbours ready to cheer you or to
fall on you, stepping delicately between the butcher
and the policeman, in the holy terror of scandal and
gallows and lunatic asylums—how can you imagine
what particular region of the first ages a man's un-
trammelled feet may take him into by the way of
solitude—utter solitude without a policeman—by the
way of silence—utter silence, where no warning voice
of a kind neighbour can be heard whispering of public
opinion? These little things make all the great difference. When they are gone you must fall back upon
your own innate strength, upon your own capacity for
faithfulness. Of course you may be too much of a fool
to go wrong—too dull even to know you are being
assaulted by the powers of darkness. I take it, no fool
ever made a bargain for his soul with the devil; the
fool is too much of a fool, or the devil too much of a
devil—I don't know which. Or you may be such a
thunderingly exalted creature as to be altogether deaf
and blind to anything but heavenly sights and sounds.
Then the earth for you is only a standing place—and
whether to be like this is your loss or your gain I
won't pretend to say. But most of us are neither one
nor the other. The earth for us is a place to live in,
where we must put up with sights, with sounds, with
smells, too, by Jove!—breathe dead hippo, so to
speak, and not be contaminated. And there, don't you
see? Your strength comes in, the faith in your ability
for the digging of unostentatious holes to bury the
stuff in—your power of devotion, not to yourself, but
to an obscure, back-breaking business. And that's difficult enough. Mind, I am not trying to excuse or even
explain—I am trying to account to myself for—for—
Mr. Kurtz—for the shade of Mr. Kurtz. This initiated
wraith from the back of Nowhere honoured me with
its amazing confidence before it vanished altogether.
This was because it could speak English to me. The
original Kurtz had been educated partly in England,

and—as he was good enough to say himself—his sympathies were in the right place. His mother was half-English, his father was half-French. All Europe contributed to the making of Kurtz; and by and by I learned that, most appropriately, the International Society for the Suppression of Savage Customs had intrusted him with the making of a report, for its future guidance. And he had written it, too. I've seen it. I've read it. It was eloquent, vibrating with eloquence, but too high-strung, I think. Seventeen pages of close writing he had found time for! But this must have been before his—let us say—nerves, went wrong, and caused him to preside at certain midnight dances ending with unspeakable rites, which—as far as I reluctantly gathered from what I heard at various times—were offered up to him—do you understand?—to Mr. Kurtz himself. But it was a beautiful piece of writing. The opening paragraph, however, in the light of later information, strikes me now as ominous. He began with the argument that we whites, from the point of development we had arrived at, 'must necessarily appear to them [savages] in the nature of supernatural beings—we approach them with the might as of a deity,' and so on, and so on. 'By the simple exercise of our will we can exert a power for good practically unbounded,' etc., etc. From that point he soared and took me with him. The peroration was magnificent, though difficult to remember, you know. It gave me the notion of an exotic Immensity ruled by an august Benevolence. It made me tingle with enthusiasm. This was the unbounded power of eloquence—of words—of burning noble words. There were no practical hints to interrupt the magic current of phrases, unless a kind of note at the foot of the last page, scrawled evidently much later, in an unsteady hand, may be regarded as the exposition of a method. It was very simple, and at the end of that moving appeal to every altruistic sentiment it blazed at you, luminous and terrifying, like a flash of lightning in a serene sky: 'Exterminate all the brutes!' The curious part was that he had apparently

forgotten all about that valuable postscriptum, because, later on, when he in a sense came to himself,
he repeatedly entreated me to take good care of 'my
pamphlet' (he called it), as it was sure to have in the
future a good influence upon his career. I had full
information about all these things, and, besides, as it
turned out, I was to have the care of his memory. I've
done enough for it to give me the indisputable right
to lay it, if I choose, for an everlasting rest in the
dust-bin of progress, amongst all the sweepings and,
figuratively speaking, all the dead cats of civilization.
But then, you see, I can't choose. He won't be forgotten. Whatever he was, he was not common. He had
the power to charm or frighten rudimentary souls into
an aggravated witch-dance in his honour; he could also
fill the small souls of the pilgrims with bitter misgiv-
ings: he had one devoted friend at least, and he had
conquered one soul in the world that was neither rudimentary nor tainted with self-seeking. No; I can't forget him, though I am not prepared to affirm the fellow
was exactly worth the life we lost in getting to him. I
missed my late helmsman awfully—I missed him even
while his body was still lying in the pilot-house. Perhaps you will think it passing strange this regret for a
savage who was no more account than a grain of sand
in a black Sahara. Well, don't you see, he had done
something, he had steered; for months I had him at
my back—a help—an instrument. It was a kind of
partnership. He steered for me—I had to look after
him, I worried about his deficiencies, and thus a subtle
bond had been created, of which I only became aware
when it was suddenly broken. And the intimate pro-
fundity of that look he gave me when he received his
hurt remains to this day in my memory—like a claim
of distant kinship affirmed in a supreme moment.

"Poor fool! If he had only left that shutter alone.
He had no restraint, no restraint—just like Kurtz—a
tree swayed by the wind. As soon as I had put on a
dry pair of slippers, I dragged him out, after first jerk-
ing the spear out of his side, which operation I confess

I performed with my eyes shut tight. His heels leaped together over the little doorstep; his shoulders were pressed to my breast; I hugged him from behind desperately. Oh! he was heavy, heavy; heavier than any man on earth, I should imagine. Then without more ado I tipped him overboard. The current snatched him as though he had been a wisp of grass, and I saw the body roll over twice before I lost sight of it for ever. All the pilgrims and the manager were then congregated on the awning-deck about the pilot-house, chattering at each other like a flock of excited magpies, and there was a scandalized murmur at my heartless promptitude. What they wanted to keep that body hanging about for I can't guess. Embalm it, maybe. But I had also heard another, and a very ominous, murmur on the deck below. My friends the woodcutters were likewise scandalized, and with a better show of reason—though I admit that the reason itself was quite inadmissible. Oh, quite! I had made up my mind that if my late helmsman was to be eaten, the fishes alone should have him. He had been a very second-rate helmsman while alive, but now he was dead he might have become a first-class temptation, and possibly cause some startling trouble. Besides, I was anxious to take the wheel, the man in pink pyjamas showing himself a hopeless duffer at the business.

"This I did directly the simple funeral was over. We were going half-speed, keeping right in the middle of the stream, and I listened to the talk about me. They had given up Kurtz, they had given up the station; Kurtz was dead, and the station had been burnt—and so on—and so on. The red-haired pilgrim was beside himself with the thought that at least this poor Kurtz had been properly avenged. 'Say! We must have made a glorious slaughter of them in the bush. Eh? What do you think? Say?' He positively danced, the bloodthirsty little gingery beggar. And he had nearly fainted when he saw the wounded man! I could not help saying, 'You made a glorious lot of smoke, anyhow.' I had seen, from the way the tops of bushes rustled and flew, that almost all the shots had gone too high. You can't hit anything unless you take aim and fire from the shoulder; but these chaps fired from the hip with their eyes shut. The retreat, I maintained—and I was right—was caused by the screeching of the steam whistle. Upon this they forgot Kurtz, and began to howl at me with indignant protests.

"The manager stood by the wheel murmuring confidentially about the necessity of getting well away down the river before dark at all events, when I saw in the distance a clearing on the riverside and the outlines of some sort of building. 'What's this?' I asked. He clapped his hands in wonder. 'The station!' he cried. I edged in at once, still going half-speed.

"Through my glasses I saw the slope of a hill interspersed with rare trees and perfectly free from undergrowth. A long decaying building on the summit was half buried in the high grass; the large holes in the peaked roof gaped black from afar; the jungle and the woods made a background. There was no enclosure or fence of any kind; but there had been one apparently, for near the house half-a-dozen slim posts remained in a row, roughly trimmed, and with their upper ends ornamented with round carved balls. The rails, or whatever there had been between, had disappeared. Of course the forest surrounded all that. The river-bank was clear, and on the waterside I saw a white man under a hat like a cart-wheel beckoning persistently with his whole arm. Examining the edge of the forest above and below, I was almost certain I could see movements—human forms gliding here and there. I steamed past prudently, then stopped the engines and let her drift down. The man on the shore began to shout, urging us to land. 'We have been attacked,' screamed the manager. 'I know—I know. It's all right,' yelled back the other, as cheerful as you please. 'Come along. It's all right. I am glad.'

"His aspect reminded me of something I had seen—something funny I had seen somewhere. As I manœuvred to get alongside, I was asking myself, 'What does

this fellow look like?' Suddenly I got it. He looked
like a harlequin. His clothes had been made of some
stuff that was brown holland probably, but it was covered with patches all over, with bright patches, blue,
red, and yellow—patches on the back, patches on the
front, patches on elbows, on knees; coloured binding
around his jacket, scarlet edging at the bottom of his
trousers; and the sunshine made him look extremely
gay and wonderfully neat withal, because you could
see how beautifully all this patching had been done.
A beardless, boyish face, very fair, no features to
speak of, nose peeling, little blue eyes, smiles and
frowns chasing each other over that open countenance
like sunshine and shadow on a wind-swept plain.
'Look out, captain!' he cried; 'there's a snag lodged
in here last night.' What! Another snag? I confess I
swore shamefully. I had nearly holed my cripple, to
finish off that charming trip. The harlequin on the
bank turned his little pug-nose up to me. 'You English?' he asked, all smiles. 'Are you?' I shouted from
the wheel. The smiles vanished, and he shook his head
as if sorry for my disappointment. Then he brightened
up. 'Never mind!' he cried encouragingly. 'Are we in
time?' I asked. 'He is up there,' he replied, with a toss
of the head up the hill, and becoming gloomy all of a
sudden. His face was like the autumn sky, overcast
one moment and bright the next.

"When the manager, escorted by the pilgrims, all of
them armed to the teeth, had gone to the house this
chap came on board. 'I say, I don't like this. These
natives are in the bush,' I said. He assured me earnestly it was all right. 'They are simple people,' he
added; 'well, I am glad you came. It took me all my
time to keep them off.' 'But you said it was all right,'
I cried. 'Oh, they meant no harm,' he said; and as I
stared he corrected himself, 'Not exactly.' Then viva-
ciously, 'My faith, your pilot-house wants a clean-up!'
In the next breath he advised me to keep enough
steam on the boiler to blow the whistle in case of any
trouble. 'One good screech will do more for you than

all your rifles. They are simple people,' he repeated.
He rattled away at such a rate he quite overwhelmed
me. He seemed to be trying to make up for lots of
silence, and actually hinted, laughing, that such was
the case. 'Don't you talk with Mr. Kurtz?' I said. 'You
don't talk with that man—you listen to him,' he exclaimed with severe exaltation. 'But now——' He
waved his arm, and in the twinkling of an eye was in
the uttermost depths of despondency. In a moment he
came up again with a jump, possessed himself of both
my hands, shook them continuously, while he gabbled:
'Brother sailor . . . honour . . . pleasure . . . delight . . .
introduce myself . . . Russian . . . son of an arch-
priest . . . Government of Tambov . . . What? Tobacco! English tobacco; the excellent English tobacco!
Now, that's brotherly. Smoke? Where's a sailor that
does not smoke?'

"The pipe soothed him, and gradually I made out
he had run away from school, had gone to sea in a
Russian ship; ran away again; served some time in
English ships; was now reconciled with the arch-priest.
He made a point of that. 'But when one is young one
must see things, gather experience, ideas; enlarge the
mind.' 'Here!' I interrupted. 'You can never tell! Here
I met Mr. Kurtz,' he said, youthfully solemn and re-
proachful. I held my tongue after that. It appears he
had persuaded a Dutch trading-house on the coast to
fit him out with stores and goods, and had started for
the interior with a light heart and no more idea of
what would happen to him than a baby. He had been
wandering about that river for nearly two years alone,
cut off from everybody and everything. 'I am not so
young as I look. I am twenty-five,' he said. 'At first
old Van Shuyten would tell me to go to the devil,' he
narrated with keen enjoyment; 'but I stuck to him,
and talked and talked, till at last he got afraid I would
talk the hind-leg off his favourite dog, so he gave me
some cheap things and a few guns, and told me he
hoped he would never see my face again. Good old
Dutchman, Van Shuyten. I've sent him one small lot

of ivory a year ago, so that he can't call me a little thief when I get back. I hope he got it. And for the rest I don't care. I had some wood stacked for you. That was my old house. Did you see?'

"I gave him Towson's book. He made as though he would kiss me, but restrained himself. 'The only book I had left, and I thought I had lost it,' he said, looking at it ecstatically. 'So many accidents happen to a man going about alone, you know. Canoes get upset sometimes— and sometimes you've got to clear out so quick when the people get angry.' He thumbed the pages. 'You made notes in Russian?' I asked. He nodded. 'I thought they were written in cipher,' I said. He laughed, then became serious. 'I had lots of trouble to keep these people off,' he said. 'Did they want to kill you?' I asked. 'Oh, no!' he cried, and checked himself. 'Why did they attack us?' I pursued. He hesitated, then said shame-facedly, 'They don't want him to go.' 'Don't they?' I said curiously. He nodded a nod full of mystery and wisdom. 'I tell you,' he cried, 'this man has enlarged my mind.' He opened his arms wide, staring at me with his little blue eyes that were perfectly round.

III

"I looked at him, lost in astonishment. There he was before me, in motley, as though he had absconded from a troupe of mimes, enthusiastic, fabulous. His very existence was improbable, inexplicable, and alto-gether bewildering. He was an insoluble problem. It was inconceivable how he had existed, how he had succeeded in getting so far, how he had managed to remain—why he did not instantly disappear. 'I went a little farther,' he said, 'then still a little farther—till I had gone so far that I don't know how I'll ever get back. Never mind. Plenty time. I can manage. You take Kurtz away quick—quick—I tell you.' The glam-our of youth enveloped his parti-coloured rags, his destitution, his loneliness, the essential desolation of

his futile wanderings. For months—for years—his life
hadn't been worth a day's purchase; and there he was
gallantly, thoughtlessly alive, to all appearance inde-
structible solely by the virtue of his few years and of
his unreflecting audacity. I was seduced into something
like admiration—like envy. Glamour urged him on,
glamour kept him unscathed. He surely wanted nothing from the wilderness but space to breathe in and
to push on through. His need was to exist, and to
move onwards at the greatest possible risk, and with
a maximum of privation. If the absolutely pure, uncal-
culating, unpractical spirit of adventure had ever ruled
a human being, it ruled this bepatched youth. I almost
envied him the possession of this modest and clear
flame. It seemed to have consumed all thought of self
so completely, that even while he was talking to you,
you forgot that it was he—the man before your eyes—
who had gone through these things. I did not envy
him his devotion to Kurtz, though. He had not medi-
tated over it. It came to him, and he accepted it with
a sort of eager fatalism. I must say that to me it appeared about the most dangerous thing in every way
he had come upon so far.

"They had come together unavoidably, like two
ships becalmed near each other, and lay rubbing sides
at last. I suppose Kurtz wanted an audience, because
on a certain occasion, when encamped in the forest,
they had talked all night, or more probably Kurtz had
talked. 'We talked of everything,' he said, quite transported at the recollection. 'I forgot there was such a
thing as sleep. The night did not seem to last an hour.
Everything! Everything! . . . Of love, too.' 'Ah, he
talked to you of love!' I said, much amused. 'It isn't
what you think,' he cried, almost passionately. 'It was
in general. He made me see things—things.'

"He threw his arms up. We were on deck at the
time, and the headman of my wood-cutters, lounging
near by, turned upon him his heavy and glittering
eyes. I looked around, and I don't know why, but I
assure you that never, never before, did this land, this

river, this jungle, the very arch of this blazing sky, appear to me so hopeless and so dark, so impenetrable to human thought, so pitiless to human weakness. 'And, ever since, you have been with him, of course?' I said.

"On the contrary. It appears their intercourse had been very much broken by various causes. He had, as he informed me proudly, managed to nurse Kurtz through two illnesses (he alluded to it as you would to some risky feat), but as a rule Kurtz wandered alone, far in the depths of the forest. 'Very often coming to this station, I had to wait days and days before he would turn up,' he said. 'Ah, it was worth waiting for!—sometimes.' 'What was he doing? exploring or what?' I asked. 'Oh, yes, of course'; he had discovered lots of villages, a lake, too—he did not know exactly in what direction; it was dangerous to inquire too much—but mostly his expeditions had been for ivory. 'But he had no goods to trade with by that time,' I objected. 'There's a good lot of cartridges left even yet,' he answered, looking away. 'To speak plainly, he raided the country,' I said. He nodded. 'Not alone, surely!' He muttered something about the villages round that lake. 'Kurtz got the tribe to follow him, did he?' I suggested. He fidgeted a little. 'They adored him,' he said. The tone of these words was so extraordinary that I looked at him searchingly. It was curious to see his mingled eagerness and reluctance to speak of Kurtz. The man filled his life, occupied his thoughts, swayed his emotions. 'What can you expect?' he burst out; 'he came to them with thunder and lightning, you know—and they had never seen anything like it—and very terrible. He could be very terrible. You can't judge Mr. Kurtz as you would an ordinary man. No, no, no! Now—just to give you an idea—I don't mind telling you, he wanted to shoot me, too, one day—but I don't judge him.' 'Shoot you!' I cried. 'What for?' 'Well, I had a small lot of ivory the chief of that village near my house gave me. You see I used to shoot game for them. Well, he wanted it, and wouldn't hear rea-

son. He declared he would shoot me unless I gave
him the ivory and then cleared out of the country,
because he could do so, and had a fancy for it, and
there was nothing on earth to prevent him killing
whom he jolly well pleased. And it was true, too. I
gave him the ivory. What did I care! But I didn't clear
out. No, no. I couldn't leave him. I had to be careful,
of course, till we got friendly again for a time. He had
his second illness then. Afterwards I had to keep out
of the way; but I didn't mind. He was living for the
most part in those villages on the lake. When he came
down to the river, sometimes he would take to me,
and sometimes it was better for me to be careful. This
man suffered too much. He hated all this, and somehow he couldn't get away. When I had a chance I
begged him to try and leave while there was time; I
offered to go back with him. And he would say yes,
and then he would remain; go off on another ivory
hunt; disappear for weeks; forget himself amongst
these people—forget himself—you know.' 'Why! he's
mad,' I said. He protested indignantly. Mr. Kurtz
couldn't be mad. If I had heard him talk, only two
days ago, I wouldn't dare hint at such a thing. . . . I
had take up my binoculars while we talked, and was
looking at the shore, sweeping the limit of the forest
at each side and at the back of the house. The consciousness of there being people in that bush, so silent,
so quiet—as silent and quiet as the ruined house on
the hill—made me uneasy. There was no sign on the
face of nature of this amazing tale that was not so
much told as suggested to me in desolate exclamations, completed by shrugs, in interrupted phrases, in
hints ending in deep sighs. The woods were unmoved,
like a mask—heavy, like the closed door of a prison—
they looked with their air of hidden knowledge, of
patient expectation, of unapproachable silence. The
Russian was explaining to me that it was only lately
that Mr. Kurtz had come down to the river, bringing
along with him all the fighting men of that lake tribe.
He had been absent for several months—getting him-

self adored, I suppose—and had come down unexpectedly, with the intention to all appearance of making
a raid either across the river or down stream. Evidently the appetite for more ivory had got the better
of the—what shall I say?—less material aspirations.
However he had got much worse suddenly. 'I heard
he was lying helpless, and so I came up—took my
chance,' said the Russian. 'Oh, he is bad, very bad.' I
directed my glass to the house. There were no signs
of life, but there was the ruined roof, the long mud
wall peeping above the grass, with three little square
window-holes, no two of the same size; all this brought
within reach of my hand, as it were. And then I made
a brusque movement, and one of the remaining posts
of that vanished fence leaped up in the field of my
glass. You remember I told you I had been struck at
the distance by certain attempts at ornamentation,
rather remarkable in the ruinous aspect of the place.
Now I had suddenly a nearer view, and its first result
was to make me throw my head back as if before a
blow. Then I went carefully from post to post with my
glass, and I saw my mistake. These round knobs were
not ornamental but symbolic; they were expressive
and puzzling, striking and disturbing—food for thought
and also for vultures if there had been any looking
down from the sky; but at all events for such ants as
were industrious enough to ascend the pole. They
would have been even more impressive, those heads
on the stakes, if their faces had not been turned to
the house. Only one, the first I had made out, was
facing my way. I was not so shocked as you may think.
The start back I had given was really nothing but a
movement of surprise. I had expected to see a knob
of wood there, you know. I returned deliberately to
the first I had seen—and there it was, black, dried,
sunken, with closed eyelids—a head that seemed to
sleep at the top of that pole, and, with the shrunken
dry lips showing a narrow white line of the teeth, was
smiling, too, smiling continuously at some endless and
jocose dream of that eternal slumber.

"I am not disclosing any trade secrets. In fact, the manager said afterwards that Mr. Kurtz's methods had ruined the district. I have no opinion on that point, but I want you clearly to understand that there was nothing exactly profitable in these heads being there. They only showed that Mr. Kurtz lacked restraint in the gratification of his various lusts, that there was something wanting in him—some small matter which, when the pressing need arose, could not be found under his magnificent eloquence. Whether he knew of this deficiency himself I can't say. I think the knowledge came to him at last—only at the very last. But the wilderness had found him out early, and had taken on him a terrible vengeance for the fantastic invasion. I think it had whispered to him things about himself which he did not know, things of which he had no conception till he took counsel with this great solitude—and the whisper had proved irresistibly fascinating. It echoed loudly within him because he was hollow at the core. . . . I put down the glass, and the head that had appeared near enough to be spoken to seemed at once to have leaped away from me into inaccessible distance.

"The admirer of Mr. Kurtz was a bit crestfallen. In a hurried, indistinct voice he began to assure me he had not dared to take these—say, symbols—down. He was not afraid of the natives; they would not stir till Mr. Kurtz gave the word. His ascendancy was extraordinary. The camps of these people surrounded the place, and the chiefs came every day to see him. They would crawl. . . . 'I don't want to know anything of the ceremonies used when approaching Mr. Kurtz,' I shouted. Curious, this feeling that came over me that such details would be more intolerable than those heads drying on the stakes under Mr. Kurtz's windows. After all, that was only a savage sight, while I seemed at one bound to have been transported into some lightless region of subtle horrors, where pure, uncomplicated savagery was a positive relief, being something that had a right to exist—obviously—in the

sunshine. The young man looked at me with surprise. I suppose it did not occur to him that Mr. Kurtz was no idol of mine. He forgot I hadn't heard any of these splendid monologues on, what was it? on love, justice, conduct of life—or what not. If it had come to crawling before Mr. Kurtz, he crawled as much as the veriest savage of them all. I had no idea of the conditions, he said: these heads were the heads of rebels. I shocked him excessively by laughing. Rebels! What would be the next definition I was to hear? There had been enemies, criminals, workers—and these were rebels. Those rebellious heads looked very subdued to me on their sticks. 'You don't know how such a life tires a man like Kurtz,' cried Kurtz's last disciple. 'Well, and you?' I said. 'I! I! I am a simple man. I have no great thoughts. I want nothing from anybody. How can you compare me to . . . ?' His feelings were too much for speech, and suddenly he broke down. 'I don't understand,' he groaned. 'I've been doing my best to keep him alive, and that's enough. I had no hand in all this. I have no abilities. There hasn't been a drop of medicine or a mouthful of invalid food for months here. He was shamefully abandoned. A man like this, with such ideas. Shamefully! Shamefully! I—I—haven't slept for the last ten nights . . .'

"His voice lost itself in the calm of the evening. The long shadows of the forest had slipped downhill while we talked, had gone far beyond the ruined hovel, beyond the symbolic row of stakes. All this was in the gloom, while we down there were yet in the sunshine, and the stretch of the river abreast of the clearing glittered in a still and dazzling splendour, with a murky and overshadowed bend above and below. Not a living soul was seen on the shore. The bushes did not rustle.

"Suddenly round the corner of the house a group of men appeared, as though they had come up from the ground. They waded waist-deep in the grass, in a compact body, bearing an improvised stretcher in their midst. Instantly, in the emptiness of the landscape, a

cry arose whose shrillness pierced the still air like a
sharp arrow flying straight to the very heart of the
land; and, as if by enchantment, streams of human
beings—of naked human beings—with spears in their
hands, with bows, with shields, with wild glances and
savage movements, were poured into the clearing by
the dark-faced and pensive forest. The bushes shook,
the grass swayed for a time, and then everything stood
still in attentive immobility.

" 'Now, if he does not say the right thing to them
we are all done for,' said the Russian at my elbow.
The knot of men with the stretcher had stopped, too,
halfway to the steamer, as if petrified. I saw the man
on the stretcher sit up, lank and with an uplifted arm,
above the shoulders of the bearers. 'Let us hope that
the man who can talk so well of love in general will
find some particular reason to spare us this time,' I
said. I resented bitterly the absurd danger of our situation, as if to be at the mercy of that atrocious phantom
had been a dishonouring necessity. I could not hear a
sound, but through my glasses I saw the thin arm extended commandingly, the lower jaw moving, the eyes
of that apparition shining darkly far in its bony head
that nodded with grotesque jerks. Kurtz—Kurtz—that
means short in German—don't it? Well, the name was
as true as everything else in life—and death. He
looked at least seven feet long. His covering had fallen
off, and his body emerged from it pitiful and appalling
as from a winding-sheet. I could see the cage of his
ribs all astir, the bones of his arm waving. It was as
though an animated image of death carved out of old
ivory had been shaking its hand with menaces at a
motionless crowd of men made of dark and glittering
bronze. I saw him open his mouth wide—it gave him
a weirdly voracious aspect, as though he had wanted
to swallow all the air, all the earth, all the men before
him. A deep voice reached me faintly. He must have
been shouting. He fell back suddenly. The stretcher
shook as the bearers staggered forward again, and almost at the same time I noticed that the crowd of

savages was vanishing without any perceptible movement of retreat, as if the forest that had ejected these beings so suddenly had drawn them in again as the breath is drawn in a long aspiration.

"Some of the pilgrims behind the stretcher carried his arms—two shot-guns, a heavy rifle, and a light revolver-carbine—the thunderbolts of that pitiful Jupiter. The manager bent over him murmuring as he walked beside his head. They laid him down in one of the little cabins—just a room for a bed place and a camp-stool or two, you know. We had brought his belated correspondence, and a lot of torn envelopes and open letters littered his bed. His hand roamed feebly amongst these papers. I was struck by the fire of his eyes and the composed languor of his expression. It was not so much the exhaustion of disease. He did not seem in pain. This shadow looked satiated and calm, as though for the moment it had had its fill of all the emotions.

"He rustled one of the letters, and looking straight in my face said, 'I am glad.' Somebody had been writing to him about me. These special recommendations were turning up again. The volume of tone he emitted without effort, almost without the trouble of moving his lips, amazed me. A voice! a voice! It was grave, profound, vibrating, while the man did not seem capable of a whisper. However, he had enough strength in him—factitious no doubt—to very nearly make an end of us, as you shall hear directly.

"The manager appeared silently in the doorway; I stepped out at once and he drew the curtain after me. The Russian, eyed curiously by the pilgrims, was staring at the shore. I followed the direction of his glance.

"Dark human shapes could be made out in the distance, flitting indistinctly against the gloomy border of the forest, and near the river two bronze figures, leaning on tall spears, stood in the sunlight under fantastic headdresses of spotted skins, warlike and still in statuesque repose. And from right to left along the lighted shore moved a wild and gorgeous apparition of a woman.

"She walked with measured steps, draped in striped and fringed cloths, treading the earth proudly, with a slight jingle and flash of barbarous ornaments. She carried her head high; her hair was done in the shape of a helmet; she had brass leggings to the knee, brass wire gauntlets to the elbow, a crimson spot on her tawny cheek, innumerable necklaces of glass beads on her neck; bizarre things, charms, gifts of witch-men, that hung about her, glittered and trembled at every step. She must have had the value of several elephant tusks upon her. She was savage and superb, wild-eyed and magnificent; there was something ominous and stately in her deliberate progress. And in the hush that had fallen suddenly upon the whole sorrowful land, the immense wilderness, the colossal body of the fecund and mysterious life seemed to look at her, pensive, as though it had been looking at the image of its own tenebrous and passionate soul.

"She came abreast of the steamer, stood still, and faced us. Her long shadow fell to the water's edge. Her face had a tragic and fierce aspect of wild sorrow and of dumb pain mingled with the fear of some struggling, half-shaped resolve. She stood looking at us without a stir, and like the wilderness itself, with an air of brooding over an inscrutable purpose. A whole minute passed, and then she made a step forward. There was a low jingle, a glint of yellow metal, a sway of fringed draperies, and she stopped as if her heart had failed her. The young fellow by my side growled. The pilgrims murmured at my back. She looked at us all as if her life had depended upon the unswerving steadiness of her glance. Suddenly she opened her bared arms and threw them up rigid above her head, as though in an uncontrollable desire to touch the sky, and at the same time the swift shadows darted out on the earth, swept around on the river, gathering the steamer into a shadowy embrace. A formidable silence hung over the scene.

"She turned away slowly, walked on, following the bank, and passed into the bushes to the left. Once only her eyes gleamed back at us in the dusk of the thickets before she disappeared.

" 'If she had offered to come aboard I really think I would have tried to shoot her,' said the man of patches, nervously. 'I have been risking my life every day for the last fortnight to keep her out of the house. She got in one day and kicked up a row about those miserable rags I picked up in the storeroom to mend my clothes with. I wasn't decent. At least it must have been that, for she talked like a fury to Kurtz for an hour, pointing at me now and then. I don't understand the dialect of this tribe. Luckily for me, I fancy Kurtz felt too ill that day to care, or there would have been mischief. I don't understand. . . . No—it's too much for me. Ah, well, it's all over now.'

"At this moment I heard Kurtz's deep voice behind the curtain: 'Save me!—save the ivory, you mean. Don't tell me. Save *me*! Why, I've had to save you. You are interrupting my plans now. Sick! Sick! Not so sick as you would like to believe. Never mind. I'll carry my ideas out yet—I will return. I'll show you what can be done. You with your little peddling notices—you are interfering with me. I will return. I. . . .'

"The manager came out. He did me the honour to take me under the arm and lead me aside. 'He is very low, very low,' he said. He considered it necessary to sigh, but neglected to be consistently sorrowful. 'We have done all we could for him—haven't we? But there is no disguising the fact, Mr. Kurtz has done more harm than good to the Company. He did not see the time was not ripe for vigorous action. Cautiously, cautiously—that's my principle. We must be cautious yet. The district is closed to us for a time. Deplorable! Upon the whole, the trade will suffer. I don't deny there is a remarkable quantity of ivory—mostly fossil. We must save it, at all events—but look how precarious the position is—and why? Because the method is unsound.' 'Do you,' said I, looking at the shore, 'call it "unsound method"?' 'Without doubt,' he exclaimed hotly. 'Don't you?' . . . 'No method at all,' I murmured after a while. 'Exactly,' he exulted. 'I anticipated this. Shows a complete want of judgment. It is my duty to point it out in the proper quarter.' 'Oh,' said I, 'that fellow—what's his name?—the brickmaker, will make a readable report for you.' He appeared confounded for a moment. It seemed to me I had never breathed an atmosphere so vile, and I turned mentally to Kurtz for relief—positively for relief. 'Nevertheless I think Mr. Kurtz is a remarkable man,' I said with emphasis. He started, dropped on me a cold heavy glance, said very quietly, 'he *was*,' and turned his back on me. My hour of favour was over; I found myself lumped along with Kurtz as a partisan of methods for which the time was not ripe: I was unsound! Ah! but it was something to have at least a choice of nightmares.

"I had turned to the wilderness really, not to Mr. Kurtz, who, I was ready to admit, was as good as buried. And for a moment it seemed to me as if I also were buried in a vast grave full of unspeakable secrets. I felt an intolerable weight oppressing my breast, the smell of the damp earth, the unseen presence of victorious corruption, the darkness of an impenetrable night. . . . The Russian tapped me on the shoulder. I heard him mumbling and stammering something about 'brother seaman—couldn't conceal—knowledge of matters that would affect Mr. Kurtz's reputation.' I waited. For him evidently Mr. Kurtz was not in his grave; I suspect that for him Mr. Kurtz was one of the immortals. "Well!" said I at last, 'speak out. As it happens, I am Mr. Kurtz's friend—in a way.'

"He stated with a good deal of formality that had we not been 'of the same profession,' he would have kept the matter to himself without regard to consequences. 'He suspected there was an active ill-will towards him on the part of these white men that—' 'You are right,' I said, remembering a certain conversation I had overheard. 'The manager thinks you ought to be hanged.' He showed a concern at this intelligence which amused me at first. 'I had better get out of the

way quietly,' he said earnestly. 'I can do no more for
Kurtz now, and they would soon find some excuse.
What's to stop them? There's a military post three
hundred miles from here.' 'Well, upon my word,' said
I, 'perhaps you had better go if you have any friends
amongst the savages near by.' 'Plenty,' he said. 'They
are simple people—and I want nothing, you know.'
He stood biting his lip, then: 'I don't want any harm
to happen to these whites here, but of course I was
thinking of Mr. Kurtz's reputation—but you are a
brother seaman and—' 'All right,' said I, after a time.
'Mr. Kurtz's reputation is safe with me.' I did not
know how truly I spoke.

"He informed me, lowering his voice, that it was
Kurtz who had ordered the attack to be made on the
steamer. 'He hated sometimes the idea of being taken
away—and then again. . . . But I don't understand
these matters. I am a simple man. He thought it would
scare you away—that you would give it up, thinking
him dead. I could not stop him. Oh, I had an awful
time of it this last month.' 'Very well,' I said. 'He is all
right now.' 'Ye-e-es,' he muttered, not very convinced
apparently. 'Thanks,' said I; 'I shall keep my eyes
open.' 'Be quiet—eh?' he urged anxiously. 'It would
be awful for his reputation if anybody here——' I
promised a complete discretion with great gravity. 'I
have a canoe and three black fellows waiting not very
far. I am off. Could you give me a few Martini-Henry
cartridges?' I could, and did, with proper secrecy. He
helped himself, with a wink at me, to a handful of my
tobacco.' 'Between sailors—you know—good English
tobacco.' At the door of the pilot-house he turned
round—'I say, haven't you a pair of shoes you could
spare?' He raised one leg. 'Look.' The soles were tied
with knotted strings sandalwise under his bare feet. I
rooted out an old pair, at which he looked with admiration before tucking it under his left arm. One of his
pockets (bright red) was bulging with cartridges, from
the other (dark blue) peeped 'Towson's Inquiry,' etc.,
etc. He seemed to think himself excellently well

equipped for a renewed encounter with the wilderness.
'Ah! I'll never, never meet such a man again. You
ought to have heard him recite poetry—his own, too,
it was, he told me. Poetry!' He rolled his eyes at the
recollection of these delights. 'Oh, he enlarged my
mind!' 'Good-bye,' said I. He shook hands and vanished in the night. Sometimes I ask myself whether I
had ever really seen him—whether it was possible to
meet such a phenomenon! . . .

"When I woke up shortly after midnight his warning
came to my mind with its hint of danger that seemed,
in the starred darkness, real enough to make me get
up for the purpose of having a look round. On the
hill a big fire burned, illuminating fitfully a crooked
corner of the station-house. One of the agents with a
picket of a few of our blacks, armed for the purpose,
was keeping guard over the ivory; but deep within the
forest, red gleams that wavered, that seemed to sink
and rise from the ground amongst confused columnar
shapes of intense blackness, showed the exact position
of the camp where Mr. Kurtz's adorers were keeping
their uneasy vigil. The monotonous beating of a big
drum filled the air with muffled shocks and a lingering
vibration. A steady droning sound of many men chant-
ing each to himself some weird incantation came out
from the black, flat wall of the woods as the humming
of bees comes out of a hive, and had a strange narcotic
effect upon my half-awake senses. I believe I dozed
off leaning over the rail, till an abrupt burst of yells, an
overwhelming outbreak of a pent-up and mysterious
frenzy, woke me up in a bewildered wonder. It was
cut short all at once, and the low droning went on
with an effect of audible and soothing silence. I
glanced casually into the little cabin. A light was burning within, but Mr. Kurtz was not there.

"I think I would have raised an outcry if I had
believed my eyes. But I didn't believe them at first—
the thing seemed so impossible. The fact is I was completely unnerved by a sheer blank fright, pure abstract
terror, unconnected with any distinct shape of physical

danger. What made this emotion so overpowering was—how shall I define it?—the moral shock I received, as if something altogether monstrous, intolerable to thought and odious to the soul, had been thrust upon me unexpectedly. This lasted of course the merest fraction of a second, and then the usual sense of commonplace, deadly danger, the possibility of a sudden onslaught and massacre, or something of the kind, which I saw impending, was positively welcome and composing. It pacified me, in fact, so much that I did not raise an alarm.

"There was an agent buttoned up inside an ulster and sleeping on a chair on deck within three feet of me. The yells had not awakened him; he snored very slightly; I left him to his slumbers and leaped ashore. I did not betray Mr. Kurtz—it was ordered I should never betray him—it was written I should be loyal to the nightmare of my choice. I was anxious to deal with this shadow by myself alone—and to this day I don't know why I was so jealous of sharing with any one the peculiar blackness of that experience.

"As soon as I got on the bank I saw a trail—a broad trail through the grass. I remember the exultation with which I said to myself, 'He can't walk—he is crawling on all-fours—I've got him.' The grass was wet with dew. I strode rapidly with clenched fists. I fancy I had some vague notion of falling upon him and giving him a drubbing. I don't know. I had some imbecile thoughts. The knitting old woman with the cat obtruded herself upon my memory as a most improper person to be sitting at the other end of such an affair. I saw a row of pilgrims squirting lead in the air out of Winchesters held to the hip. I thought I would never get back to the steamer, and imagined myself living alone and unarmed in the woods to an advanced age. Such silly things—you know. And I remember I confounded the beat of the drum with the beating of my heart, and was pleased at its calm regularity.

"I kept to the track though—then stopped to listen. The night was very clear; a dark blue space, sparkling with dew and starlight, in which black things stood very still. I thought I could see a kind of motion ahead of me. I was strangely cocksure of everything that night. I actually left the track and ran in a wide semi-circle (I verily believe chuckling to myself) so as to get in front of that stir, of that motion I had seen—if indeed I had seen anything. I was circumventing Kurtz as though it had been a boyish game.

"I came upon him, and if he had not heard me coming, I would have fallen over him, too, but he got up in time. He rose, unsteady, long, pale, indistinct, like a vapour exhaled by the earth, and swayed slightly, misty and silent before me; while at my back the fires loomed between the trees, and the murmur of many voices issued from the forest. I had cut him off cleverly; but when actually confronting him I seemed to come to my senses, I saw the danger in its right proportion. It was by no means over yet. Suppose he began to shout? Though he could hardly stand, there was still plenty of vigour in his voice. 'Go away—hide yourself,' he said, in that profound tone. It was very awful. I glanced back. We were within thirty yards from the nearest fire. A black figure stood up, strode on long black legs, waving long black arms, across the glow. It had horns—antelope horns, I think—on its head. Some sorcerer, some witch-man, no doubt: it looked fiendlike enough. 'Do you know what you are doing?' I whispered. 'Perfectly,' he answered, raising his voice for that single word: it sounded to me far off and yet loud, like a hail through a speaking-trumpet. 'If he makes a row we are lost,' I thought to myself. This clearly was not a case for fisticuffs, even apart from the very natural aversion I had to beat that Shadow—this wandering and tormented thing. 'You will be lost,' I said—'utterly lost.' One gets sometimes such a flash of inspiration, you know. I did say the right thing, though indeed he could not have been more irretrievably lost than he was at this very moment, when the foundations of our inti-

macy were being laid—to endure—to endure—even
to the end—even beyond.

   " 'I had immense plans,' he muttered irresolutely.
'Yes,' said I; 'but if you try to shout I'll smash your
head with——' There was not a stick or a stone near.
'I will throttle you for good,' I corrected myself. 'I
was on the threshold of great things,' he pleaded, in
a voice of longing, with a wistfulness of tone that made
my blood run cold. 'And now for this stupid scoundrel——' 'Your success in Europe is assured in any
case,' I affirmed steadily. I did not want to have the
throttling of him, you understand—and indeed it
would have been very little use for any practical purpose. I tried to break the spell—the heavy, mute spell
of the wilderness—that seemed to draw him to its pitiless breast by the awakening of forgotten and brutal
instincts, by the memory of gratified and monstrous
passions. This alone, I was convinced, had driven him
out to the edge of the forest, to the bush, towards the
gleam of fires, the throb of drums, the drone of weird
incantations; this alone had beguiled his unlawful soul
beyond the bounds of permitted aspirations. And,
don't you see, the terror of the position was not in
being knocked on the head—though I had a very
lively sense of that danger, too—but in this, that I had
to deal with a being to whom I could not appeal in
the name of anything high or low. I had, even like the
niggers, to invoke him—himself—his own exalted and
incredible degradation. There was nothing either
above or below him, and I knew it. He had kicked
himself loose of the earth. Confound the man! he had
kicked the very earth to pieces. He was alone, and I
before him did not know whether I stood on the
ground or floated in the air. I've been telling you what
we said—repeating the phrases we pronounced—but
what's the good? They were common everyday words—
the familiar, vague sounds exchanged on every waking
day of life. But what of that? They had behind them,
to my mind, the terrific suggestiveness of words heard

in dreams, of phrases spoken in nightmares. Soul! If anybody ever struggled with a soul, I am the man. And I wasn't arguing with a lunatic either. Believe me or not, his intelligence was perfectly clear—concentrated, it is true, upon himself with horrible intensity, yet clear; and therein was my only chance—barring, of course, the killing him there and then, which wasn't so good, on account of unavoidable noise. But his soul was mad. Being alone in the wilderness, it had looked within itself, and, by heavens! I tell you, it had gone mad. I had—for my sins, I suppose—to go through the ordeal of looking into it myself. No eloquence could have been so withering to one's belief in mankind as his final burst of sincerity. He struggled with himself, too. I saw it—I heard it. I saw the inconceivable mystery of a soul that knew no restraint, no faith, and no fear, yet struggling blindly with itself. I kept my head pretty well; but when I had him at last stretched on the couch, I wiped my forehead, while my legs shook under me as though I had carried half a ton on my back down that hill. And yet I had only supported him, his bony arm clasped round my neck— and he was not much heavier than a child.

"When next day we left at noon, the crowd, of whose presence behind the curtain of trees I had been acutely conscious all the time, flowed out of the woods again, filled the clearing, covered the slope with a mass of naked, breathing, quivering, bronze bodies. I steamed up a bit, then swung down stream, and two thousand eyes followed the evolutions of the splashing, thumping, fierce river-demon beating the water with its terrible tail and breathing black smoke into the air. In front of the first rank, along the river, three men, plastered with bright red earth from head to foot, strutted to and fro restlessly. When we came abreast again, they faced the river, stamped their feet, nodded their horned heads, swayed their scarlet bodies; they shook towards the fierce river-demon a bunch of black feathers, a mangy skin with a pendent tail— something that looked like a dried gourd; they shouted

periodically together strings of amazing words that resembled no sounds of human language; and the deep
murmurs of the crowd, interrupted suddenly, were like
the responses of some satanic litany.

"We had carried Kurtz into the pilot-house: there
was more air there. Lying on the couch, he stared
through the open shutter. There was an eddy in the
mass of human bodies, and the woman with helmeted
head and tawny cheeks rushed out to the very brink of
the stream. She put out her hands, shouted something,
and all that wild mob took up the shout in a roaring
chorus of articulated, rapid, breathless utterance.

" 'Do you understand this?' I asked.

"He kept on looking out past me with fiery, longing
eyes, with a mingled expression of wistfulness and
hate. He made no answer, but I saw a smile, a smile
of indefinable meaning, appear on his colourless lips
that a moment after twitched convulsively. 'Do I not?'
he said slowly, gasping, as if the words had been torn
out of him by a supernatural power.

"I pulled the string of the whistle, and I did this
because I saw the pilgrims on deck getting out their
rifles with an air of anticipating a jolly lark. At the
sudden screech there was a movement of abject terror
through that wedged mass of bodies. 'Don't! don't you
frighten them away,' cried some one on deck disconso-
lately. I pulled the string time after time. They broke
and ran, they leaped, they crouched, they swerved,
they dodged the flying terror of the sound. The three
red chaps had fallen flat, face down on the shore, as
though they had been shot dead. Only the barbarous
and superb woman did not so much as flinch, and
stretched tragically her bare arms after us over the
sombre and glittering river.

"And then that imbecile crowd down on the deck
started their little fun, and I could see nothing more
for smoke.

"The brown current ran swiftly out of the heart of
darkness, bearing us down towards the sea with twice

the speed of our upward progress; and Kurtz's life was
running swiftly, too, ebbing, ebbing out of his heart
into the sea of inexorable time. The manager was very
placid, he had no vital anxieties now, he took us both
in with a comprehensive and satisfied glance: the 'affair' had come off as well as could be wished. I saw
the time approaching when I would be left alone of
the party of 'unsound method.' The pilgrims looked
upon me with disfavour. I was, so to speak, numbered
with the dead. It is strange how I accepted this unfore-
seen partnership, this choice of nightmares forced
upon me in the tenebrous land invaded by these mean
and greedy phantoms.

"Kurtz discoursed. A voice! a voice! It rang deep
to the very last. It survived his strength to hide in the
magnificent folds of eloquence the barren darkness of
his heart. Oh, he struggled! he struggled! The wastes
of his weary brain were haunted by shadowy images
now—images of wealth and fame revolving obsequi-
ously round his unextinguishable gift of noble and
lofty expression. My Intended, my station, my career,
my ideas—these were the subjects for the occasional
utterances of elevated sentiments. The shade of the
original Kurtz frequented the bedside of the hollow
sham, whose fate it was to be buried presently in the
mould of primeval earth. But both the diabolic love and
the unearthly hate of the mysteries it had penetrated
fought for the possession of that soul satiated with primitive emotions, avid of lying fame, of sham distinction,
of all the appearances of success and power.

"Sometimes he was contemptibly childish. He desired to have kings meet him at railway-stations on
his return from some ghastly Nowhere, where he intended to accomplish great things. 'You show them
you have in you something that is really profitable,
and then there will be no limits to the recognition of
your ability,' he would say. 'Of course you must take
care of the motives—right motives—always.' The long
reaches that were like one and the same reach, monotonous bends that were exactly alike, slipped past the

steamer with their multitude of secular trees looking
patiently after this grimy fragment of another world,
the forerunner of change, of conquest, of trade, of
massacres, of blessings. I looked ahead—piloting.
'Close the shutter,' said Kurtz suddenly one day; 'I
can't bear to look at this.' I did so. There was a silence. 'Oh, but I will wring your heart yet!' he cried
at the invisible wilderness.

"We broke down—as I had expected—and had to
lie up for repairs at the head of an island. This delay
was the first thing that shook Kurtz's confidence. One
morning he gave me a packet of papers and a
photograph—the lot tied together with a shoe-string.
'Keep this for me,' he said. 'This noxious fool' (meaning the manager) 'is capable of prying into my boxes
when I am not looking.' In the afternoon I saw him.
He was lying on his back with closed eyes, and I withdrew quietly, but I heard him mutter, 'Live rightly,
die, die . . .' I listened. There was nothing more. Was
he rehearsing some speech in his sleep, or was it a
fragment of a phrase from some newspaper article?
He had been writing for the papers and meant to do
so again, 'for the furthering of my ideas. It's a duty.'

"His was an impenetrable darkness. I looked at him
as you peer down at a man who is lying at the bottom
of a precipice where the sun never shines. But I had
not much time to give him, because I was helping the
engine-driver to take to pieces the leaky cylinders, to
straighten a bent connecting-rod, and in other such
matters. I lived in an infernal mess of rust, filings,
nuts, bolts, spanners, hammers, ratchet-drills—things I
abominate, because I don't get on with them. I tended
the little forge we fortunately had aboard; I toiled
wearily in a wretched scrap-heap—unless I had the
shakes too bad to stand.

"One evening coming in with a candle I was startled
to hear him say a little tremulously, 'I am lying here
in the dark waiting for death.' The light was within a
foot of his eyes. I forced myself to murmur, 'Oh, non-
sense!' and stood over him as if transfixed.

"Anything approaching the change that came over his features I have never seen before, and hope never to see again. Oh, I wasn't touched. I was fascinated. It was as though a veil had been rent. I saw on that ivory face the expression of sombre pride, of ruthless power, of craven terror—of an intense and hopeless despair. Did he live his life again in every detail of desire, temptation, and surrender during that supreme moment of complete knowledge? He cried in a whisper at some image, at some vision—he cried out twice, a cry that was no more than a breath:

" 'The horror! The horror!'

"I blew the candle out and left the cabin. The pilgrims were dining in the mess-room, and I took my place opposite the manager, who lifted his eyes to give me a questioning glance, which I successfully ignored. He leaned back, serene, with that peculiar smile of his sealing the unexpressed depths of his meanness. A continuous shower of small flies streamed upon the lamp, upon the cloth, upon our hands and faces. Suddenly the manager's boy put his insolent black head in the doorway, and said in a tone of scathing contempt:

" 'Mistah Kurtz—he dead.'

"All the pilgrims rushed out to see. I remained, and went on with my dinner. I believe I was considered brutally callous. However, I did not eat much. There was a lamp in there—light, don't you know—and outside it was so beastly, beastly dark. I went no more near the remarkable man who had pronounced a judgment upon the adventures of his soul on this earth. The voice was gone. What else had been there? But I am of course aware that next day the pilgrims buried something in a muddy hole.

"And then they very nearly buried me.

"However, as you see, I did not go to join Kurtz there and then. I did not. I remained to dream the nightmare out to the end, and to show my loyalty to Kurtz once more. Destiny. My destiny! Droll thing life is—that mysterious arrangement of merciless logic for a futile purpose. The most you can hope from it is

some knowledge of yourself—that comes too late—a
crop of unextinguishable regrets. I have wrestled with
death. It is the most unexciting contest you can imagine. It takes place in an impalpable greyness, with
nothing underfoot, with nothing around, without spectators, without clamour, without glory, without the
great desire of victory, without the great fear of de-
feat, in a sickly atmosphere of tepid skepticism, without much belief in your own right, and still less in
that of your adversary. If such is the form of ultimate
wisdom, then life is a greater riddle than some of us
think it to be. I was within a hair's breadth of the
last opportunity of pronouncement, and I found with
humiliation that probably I would have nothing to say.
This is the reason why I affirm that Kurtz was a remarkable man. He had something to say. He said it.
Since I had peeped over the edge myself, I understand
better the meaning of his stare, that could not see the
flame of the candle, but was wide enough to embrace
the whole universe, piercing enough to penetrate all
the hearts that beat in the darkness. He had summed
up—he had judged. 'The horror!' He was a remarkable man. After all, this was the expression of some
sort of belief; it had candour, it had conviction, it had
a vibrating note of revolt in its whisper, it had the
appalling face of a glimpsed truth—the strange commingling of desire and hate. And it is not my own
extremity I remember best—a vision of greyness without form filled with physical pain, and a careless contempt for the evanescence of all things—even of this
pain itself. No! It is his extremity that I seem to have
lived through. True, he had made that last stride, he
had stepped over the edge, while I had been permitted
to draw back my hesitating foot. And perhaps in this
is the whole difference; perhaps all the wisdom, and
all truth, and all sincerity, are just compressed into
that inappreciable moment of time in which we step
over the threshold of the invisible. Perhaps! I like to
think my summing-up would not have been a word of
careless contempt. Better his cry—much better. It was

an affirmation, a moral victory paid for by innumerable defeats, by abominable terrors, by abominable satisfactions. But it was a victory! That is why I have remained loyal to Kurtz to the last, and even beyond, when a long time after I heard once more, not his own voice, but the echo of his magnificent eloquence thrown to me from a soul as translucently pure as a cliff of crystal.

"No, they did not bury me, though there is a period of time which I remember mistily, with a shuddering wonder, like a passage through some inconceivable world that had no hope in it and no desire. I found myself back in the sepulchral city resenting the sight of people hurrying through the streets to filch a little money from each other, to devour their infamous cookery, to gulp their unwholesome beer, to dream their insignificant and silly dreams. They trespassed upon my thoughts. They were intruders whose knowledge of life was to me an irritating pretence, because I felt so sure they could not possibly know the things I knew. Their bearing, which was simply the bearing of commonplace individuals going about their business in the assurance of perfect safety, was offensive to me like the outrageous flauntings of folly in the face of a danger it is unable to comprehend. I had no particular desire to enlighten them, but I had some difficulty in restraining myself from laughing in their faces so full of stupid importance. I daresay I was not very well at that time. I tottered about the streets—there were various affairs to settle—grinning bitterly at perfectly respectable persons. I admit my behaviour was inexcusable, but then my temperature was seldom normal in these days. My dear aunt's endeavours to 'nurse up my strength' seemed altogether beside the mark. It was not my strength that wanted nursing, it was my imagination that wanted soothing. I kept the bundle of papers given me by Kurtz, not knowing exactly what to do with it. His mother had died lately, watched over, as I was told, by his Intended. A clean-shaved man, with an official manner and wearing gold-rimmed spectacles, called on me one day and made inquiries, at first circuitous, afterwards suavely pressing, about what he was pleased to denominate certain 'documents.' I was not surprised, because I had had two rows with the manager on the subject out there. I had refused to give up the smallest scrap out of that package, and I took the same attitude with the spectacled man. He became darkly menacing at last, and with much heat argued that the Company had the right to every bit of information about its 'territories.' And said he, 'Mr. Kurtz's knowledge of unexplored regions must have been necessarily extensive and peculiar—owing to his great abilities and to the deplorable circumstances in which he had been placed: therefore——' I assured him Mr. Kurtz's knowledge, however extensive, did not bear upon the problems of commerce or administration. He invoked then the name of science. 'It would be an incalculable loss if,' etc., etc. I offered him the report on the 'Suppression of Savage Customs,' with the postscriptum torn off. He took it up eagerly, but ended by sniffing at it with an air of contempt. 'This is not what we had a right to expect,' he remarked. 'Expect nothing else,' I said. 'There are only private letters.' He withdrew upon some threat of legal proceedings, and I saw him no more; but another fellow, calling himself Kurtz's cousin, appeared two days later, and was anxious to hear all the details about his dear relative's last moments. Incidentally he gave me to understand that Kurtz had been essentially a great musician. 'There was the making of an immense success,' said the man, who was an organist, I believe, with lank grey hair flowing over a greasy coat-collar. I had no reason to doubt this statement; and to this day I am unable to say what was Kurtz's profession, whether he ever had any—which was the greatest of his talents. I had taken him for a painter who wrote for the papers, or else for a journalist who could paint—but even the cousin (who took snuff during the interview) could not tell me what he had been— exactly. He was a universal genius—on that point I

agreed with the old chap, who thereupon blew his
nose noisily into a large cotton handkerchief and withdrew in senile agitation, bearing off some family letters and memoranda without importance. Ultimately
a journalist anxious to know something of the fate of
his 'dear colleague' turned up. This visitor informed
me Kurtz's proper sphere ought to have been politics
'on the popular side.' He had furry straight eyebrows,
bristly hair cropped short, an eyeglass on a broad rib-
bon, and, becoming expansive, confessed his opinion
that Kurtz really couldn't write a bit—'but heavens!
how that man could talk. He electrified large meetings.
He had faith—don't you see?—he had the faith. He
could get himself to believe anything—anything. He
would have been a splendid leader of an extreme
party.' 'What party?' I asked. 'Any party,' answered
the other. 'He was an—an—extremist.' Did I not think
so? I assented. Did I know, he asked, with a sudden
flash of curiosity, 'what it was that had induced him
to go out there?' 'Yes,' said I, and forthwith handed
him the famous Report for publication, if he thought
fit. He glanced through it hurriedly, mumbling all the
time, judged "it would do,' and took himself off with
this plunder.

"Thus I was left at last with a slim packet of letters
and the girl's portrait. She struck me as beautiful—I
mean she had a beautiful expression. I know that the
sunlight can be made to lie, too, yet one felt that no
manipulation of light and pose could have conveyed
the delicate shade of truthfulness upon those features.
She seemed ready to listen without mental reservation,
without suspicion, without a thought for herself. I concluded I would go and give her back her portrait and
those letters myself. Curiosity? Yes; and also some
other feeling perhaps. All that had been Kurtz's had
passed out of my hands: his soul, his body, his station,
his plans, his ivory, his career. There remained only
his memory and his Intended—and I wanted to give
that up, too, to the past, in a way—to surrender per-

sonally all that remained of him with me to that oblivion which is the last word of our common fate. I don't defend myself. I had no clear perception of what it was I really wanted. Perhaps it was an impulse of unconscious loyalty, or the fulfilment of one of those ironic necessities that lurk in the facts of human existence. I don't know. I can't tell. But I went.

"I thought his memory was like the other memories of the dead that accumulate in every man's life—a vague impress on the brain of shadows that had fallen on it in their swift and final passage; but before the high and ponderous door, between the tall houses of a street as still and decorous as a well-kept alley in a cemetery, I had a vision of him on the stretcher, opening his mouth voraciously, as if to devour all the earth with all its mankind. He lived then before me; he lived as much as he had ever lived—a shadow insatiable of splendid appearances, of frightful realities; a shadow darker than the shadow of the night, and draped nobly in the folds of a gorgeous eloquence. The vision seemed to enter the house with me—the stretcher, the phantom-bearers, the wild crowd of obedient worshippers, the gloom of the forests, the glitter of the reach between the murky bends, the beat of the drum, regular and muffled like the beating of a heart—the heart of a conquering darkness. It was a moment of triumph for the wilderness, an invading and vengeful rush which, it seemed to me, I would have to keep back alone for the salvation of another soul. And the memory of what I had heard him say afar there, with the horned shapes stirring at my back, in the glow of fires, within the patient woods, those broken phrases came back to me, were heard again in their ominous and terrifying simplicity. I remembered his abject pleading, his abject threats, the colossal scale of his vile desires, the meanness, the torment, the tempestuous anguish of his soul. And later on I seemed to see his collected languid manner, when he said one day, 'This lot of ivory now is really mine. The Company did not pay for it. I collected it myself at a very great personal risk. I am afraid they will try to claim it as theirs though. H'm. It is a difficult case. What do you think I ought to do—resist? Eh? I want no more than justice.' . . . He wanted no more than justice—no more than justice. I rang the bell before a mahogany door on the first floor, and while I waited he seemed to stare at me out of the glassy panel—stare with that wide and immense stare embracing, condemning, loathing all the universe. I seemed to hear the whispered cry, 'The horror! The horror!'

"The dusk was falling. I had to wait in a lofty drawing-room with three long windows from floor to ceiling that were like three luminous and bedraped columns. The bent gilt legs and backs of the furniture shone in indistinct curves. The tall marble fireplace had a cold and monumental whiteness. A grand piano stood massively in a corner; with dark gleams on the flat surfaces like a sombre and polished sarcophagus. A high door opened—closed. I rose.

"She came forward, all in black, with a pale head, floating towards me in the dusk. She was in mourning. It was more than a year since his death, more than a year since the news came; she seemed as though she would remember and mourn forever. She took both my hands in hers and murmured, 'I had heard you were coming.' I noticed she was not very young—I mean not girlish. She had a mature capacity for fidelity, for belief, for suffering. The room seemed to have grown darker, as if all the sad light of the cloudy evening had taken refuge on her forehead. This fair hair, this pale visage, this pure brow, seemed surrounded by an ashy halo from which the dark eyes looked out at me. Their glance was guileless, profound, confident, and trustful. She carried her sorrowful head as though she were proud of that sorrow, as though she would say, 'I—I alone knew how to mourn for him as he deserves.' But while we were still shaking hands, such a look of awful desolation came upon her face that I perceived she was one of those creatures that are not the playthings of Time. For her he had died only yesterday. And, by Jove! the impression was so powerful that for me, too, he seemed to have died only yesterday—nay, this very minute. I saw her and him in the same instant of time—his death and her sorrow—I saw her sorrow in the very moment of his death. Do you understand? I saw them together—I heard them together. She had said, with a deep catch of the breath, 'I have survived' while my strained ears seemed to hear distinctly, mingled with her tone of despairing regret, the summing up whisper of his eternal condemnation. I asked myself what I was doing there, with a sensation of panic in my heart as though I had blundered into a place of cruel and absurd mysteries not fit for a human being to behold. She motioned me to a chair. We sat down. I laid the packet gently on the little table, and she put her hand over it. . . . 'You knew him well,' she murmured, after a moment of mourning silence.

" 'Intimacy grows quickly out there,' I said. 'I knew him as well as it is possible for one man to know another.'

" 'And you admired him,' she said. 'It was impossible to know him and not to admire him. Was it?'

" 'He was a remarkable man,' I said, unsteadily. Then before the appealing fixity of her gaze, that seemed to watch for more words on my lips, I went on, 'It was impossible not to——'

" 'Love him,' she finished eagerly, silencing me into an appalled dumbness. 'How true! how true! But when you think that no one knew him so well as I! I had all his noble confidence. I knew him best.'

" 'You knew him best,' I repeated. And perhaps she did. But with every word spoken the room was growing darker, and only her forehead, smooth and white, remained illumined by the unextinguishable light of belief and love.

" 'You were his friend,' she went on. 'His friend,' she repeated, a little louder. 'You must have been, if he had given you this, and sent you to me. I feel I can speak to you—and oh! I must speak. I want you—

you who have heard his last words—to know I have been worthy of him. . . . It is not pride. . . . Yes! I am proud to know I understood him better than any one on earth—he told me so himself. And since his mother died I have had no one—no one—to—to—'

"I listened. The darkness deepened. I was not even sure whether he had given me the right bundle. I rather suspect he wanted me to take care of another batch of his papers which, after his death, I saw the manager examining under the lamp. And the girl talked, easing her pain in the certitude of my sympathy; she talked as thirsty men drink. I had heard that her engagement with Kurtz had been disapproved by her people. He wasn't rich enough or something. And indeed I don't know whether he had not been a pauper all his life. He had given me some reason to infer that it was his impatience of comparative poverty that drove him out there.

" '. . . Who was not his friend who had heard him speak once?' she was saying. 'He drew men towards him by what was best in them.' She looked at me with intensity. 'It is the gift of the great,' she went on, and the sound of her low voice seemed to have the accompaniment of all the other sounds, full of mystery, desolation, and sorrow, I had ever heard—the ripple of the river, the soughing of the trees swayed by the wind, the murmurs of the crowds, the faint ring of incomprehensible words cried from afar, the whisper of a voice speaking from beyond the threshold of an eternal darkness. 'But you have heard him! You know!' she cried.

" 'Yes, I know,' I said with something like despair in my heart, but bowing my head before the faith that was in her, before that great and saving illusion that shone with an unearthly glow in the darkness, in the triumphant darkness from which I could not have defended her—from which I could not even defend myself.

" 'What a loss to me—to us!'—she corrected herself with beautiful generosity; then added in a murmur, 'To the world.' By the last gleams of twilight I could see the glitter of her eyes, full of tears—of tears that would not fall.

"'I have been very happy—very fortunate—very proud,' she went on. 'Too fortunate. Too happy for a little while. And now I am unhappy for—for life.'

"She stood up; her fair hair seemed to catch all the remaining light in a glimmer of gold. I rose, too.

"'And of all this,' she went on mournfully, 'of all his promise, and of all his greatness, of his generous mind, of his noble heart, nothing remains—nothing but a memory. You and I——'

"'We shall always remember him,' I said hastily.

"'No!' she cried. 'It is impossible that all this should be lost—that such a life should be sacrificed to leave nothing—but sorrow. You know what vast plans he had. I knew of them, too—I could not perhaps understand—but others knew of them. Something must remain. His words, at least, have not died.'

"'His words will remain,' I said.

"'And his example,' she whispered to herself. 'Men looked up to him—his goodness shone in every act. His example——'

"'True,' I said; 'his example, too. Yes, his example. I forgot that.'

"'But I do not. I cannot—I cannot believe—not yet. I cannot believe that I shall never see him again, that nobody will see him again, never, never, never.'

"She put out her arms as if after a retreating figure, stretching them back and with clasped pale hands across the fading and narrow sheen of the window. Never see him! I saw him clearly enough then. I shall see this eloquent phantom as long as I live, and I shall see her, too, a tragic and familiar Shade, resembling in this gesture another one, tragic also, and bedecked with powerless charms, stretching bare brown arms over the glitter of the infernal stream, the stream of darkness. She said suddenly very low, 'He died as he lived.'

"'His end,' said I, with dull anger stirring in me, 'was in every way worthy of his life.'

" 'And I was not with him,' she murmured. My anger subsided before a feeling of infinite pity.

" 'Everything that could be done——' I mumbled.

" 'Ah, but I believed in him more than any one on earth—more than his own mother, more than—himself. He needed me! Me! I would have treasured every sigh, every word, every sign, every glance.'

"I felt like a chill grip on my chest. 'Don't,' I said, in a muffled voice.

" 'Forgive me. I—I have mourned so long in silence—in silence. . . . You were with him—to the last? I think of his loneliness. Nobody near to understand him as I would have understood. Perhaps no one to hear. . . .'

" 'To the very end,' I said, shakily. 'I heard his very last words. . . .' I stopped in a fright.

" 'Repeat them,' she murmured in a heart-broken tone. 'I want—I want—something—something—to—to live with.'

"I was on the point of crying at her, 'Don't you hear them?' The dusk was repeating them in a persistent whisper all around us, in a whisper that seemed to swell menacingly like the first whisper of a rising wind. 'The horror! The horror!'

" 'His last word—to live with,' she insisted. 'Don't you understand I loved him—I loved him—I loved him!'

"I pulled myself together and spoke slowly.

" 'The last words he pronounced was—your name.'

"I heard a light sigh and then my heart stood still, stopped dead short by an exulting and terrible cry, by the cry of inconceivable triumph and of unspeakable pain. 'I knew it—I was sure!' . . . She knew. She was sure. I heard her weeping; she had hidden her face in her hands. It seemed to me that the house would collapse before I could escape, that the heavens would fall upon my head. But nothing happened. The heavens do not fall for such a trifle. Would they have fallen, I wonder, if I had rendered Kurtz that justice which was his due? Hadn't he said he wanted only justice? But I couldn't. I could not tell her. It would have been too dark—too dark altogether. . . ."

Marlow ceased, and sat apart, indistinct and silent, in the pose of a meditating Buddha. Nobody moved for a time. "We have lost the first of the ebb," said the Director suddenly. I raised my head. The offing was barred by a black bank of clouds, and the tranquil waterway leading to the uttermost ends of the earth flowed sombre under an overcast sky—seemed to lead into the heart of an immense darkness.

Afterword

In the summer of 1978 I came into possession of the Signet edition of *Heart of Darkness* and *The Secret Sharer*, an earlier version of the one I presume the reader has just finished. It was green and battered and had someone else's annoying writing in the margins. The introduction to that edition was written in 1950, by Albert Guerard, who, along with his colleague at Stanford, Ian Watt, was one of the great early Conrad scholars and who did much to revive Conrad's popularity and reputation after it had fallen into a certain degree of obscurity in the middle of the century.

At the time, I was twenty years old, a sophomore at Columbia University, and I had set out specifically to read *Heart of Darkness* because when I'd read it as an assignment in high school, I'd had some difficulty understanding it. Although it is short, only a hundred pages or so in this and most other editions, *Heart of Darkness* is one of Conrad's most dense narratives. The structure of the book is complex, Conrad's irony is thick and relentless, and his language is difficult as well: he had learned English while living in France and his version of it would always be heavy with Latinates. As is often the case with Conrad, his point—his meaning or his multiple meanings—is a little hard to pick out from amid the somber moods and romantic outpourings of his narrative voice.

Yet I knew something important was there. So I

was rereading it, sitting in the lobby of a building on Morningside Drive in New York City. Columbia owned the building and it housed many of the university's most distinguished faculty members—I'd been handed a job that summer as a replacement for the union doormen of that building, taking their shifts when they went on holiday. On this particular occasion, it was midafternoon on a mild day in July. The wide lobby doors were swung open to let in the air, and the bright summer light was cheerfully lacking the mean white glare so common during New York's overbearing summers. In strolled a handsome, well-built man I recognized as Professor Edward Said, of Columbia's English department. The foregoing sentence, and that he lived on the fourth floor of this building, constituted everything I then knew about him. The book that would make him truly famous, *Orientalism*, would not come out until later that year.

He walked toward me across the long lobby and I got up, put down my book, and started over to where the elevator was located, on the north side of the building, as it was also my job to run the manual elevator. Said had a sometimes gruff and always, in those days, physically confident air with strangers; he had barely spoken to me in the past. But suddenly he was interested. "What are you reading?" he practically shouted and strode over to the table where I'd laid my book. *"Heart of Darkness!"* he said. "Great book, great book." Little did I know, from this relatively generic reaction, that Said was a respected Conrad scholar himself, that he'd done his doctoral dissertation on Conrad, that Conrad's exile and the effect it had on his personality and his work would be a source of continuing fascination for Said, nor, finally, that Conrad would be an author, and *Heart of Darkness* a text, that Said would return to over and over as he explored the fine mechanisms connecting the most transcendent art with specific cultures in specific historical situations.

We rode up to his floor and he quizzed me about what

I'd studied and read, and he urged me to take his course that fall called "Modern British Literature," where we'd read *Heart of Darkness*, among many other major late-nineteenth-century and early-twentieth-century British texts. I can say now with clarity that this limited exchange in that creaking and clanging old elevator, the four subsequent courses I took with Said, and his friendship in later years, were the most important professional influences of my life. Said was the greatest literary mind I have ever been in the presence of, by several orders of magnitude, and I would not be the critic and the writer I am without having known him and studied with him—all because of a little green book from Signet.

This personal anecdote has a powerful relevance to Conrad's work, it seems to me. The two tales you have found in this book were written ten years apart (*Heart of Darkness* was written in 1899, and *The Secret Sharer* a decade later) and they differ markedly in style, yet they are connected by virtue of sharing one of Conrad's most crucial themes: a haunting and accidental union between two people who by all rights should never have met, and who have—often incomprehensibly—the power to change each other in radical ways.

Conrad leaves a deep mystery at the core of the special relationships that drive these two tales. We are never directly instructed as to why the Captain feels such a deep kinship with Leggatt, his "secret sharer"; even more difficult to fathom is Marlow's psychological imprisonment within the ineffable relationship he forms during his brief exposure to the monstrous Kurtz. Indeed, the great challenge with which Conrad leaves us, as readers, is to come to some sort of conclusion on our own about these dark intimacies, to figure out what happens inside a person's consciousness when he is altered by the personality of someone else.

These relationships are vague in origins but quite tangible on the page. While Leggatt is still clinging to the ship's ladder and glowing with the natural phosphorus of the sea, our unnamed Captain remarks that "a mysterious communication was already established between us two." This mysterious communication will lead the Captain first to extend toward Leggatt a puzzling degree of blind trust and second to take extraordinary risks on his behalf.

Similarly, on meeting Kurtz (who is, like Leggatt, a murderer, but on a far larger and more ferocious scale), Marlow finds himself inexplicably drawn to him. "The volume of tone he emitted without effort, almost without the trouble of moving his lips, amazed me. A voice! A voice! It was grave, profound, vibrating, while the man did not seem capable of a whisper." (Notice that, as with all subsequent descriptions of his exchanges with Kurtz, Marlow reveals almost nothing of the actual content of the conversation.) Just after this first meeting, Marlow is approached by the loathsome company manager, whom we might call a petty bureaucrat supervising the plunder and rape of a continent and who wishes to go on record as deploring Kurtz's "unsound methods," even as he profits by them. Marlow recalls with disgust that he "had never breathed an atmosphere so vile, and I turned mentally to Kurtz for relief—positively for relief."

In both stories, then, we see formed a profound bond based on little available information or personal context, but rather some invisible but irresistible moral imperative, some core and highly mysterious requirement of being human. Written very close on the heels of *Heart of Darkness*, Conrad's great novel *Lord Jim*—which also features Marlow as narrator—has a moment that sums up this mystery in a brilliant and almost incoherent and wordless moment. Jim, a criminal like Leggatt and Kurtz, comes to understand the bond that has formed between Marlow and himself, and all that Marlow has done for him, and he stutters, in shock, "I—you—I . . . ." These might be the three words and two dashes that in all of Conrad best evoke his central artistic and moral concern.

*   *   *

If we are going to understand the bond between these figures, it is important to look at how the stories are told. *The Secret Sharer* is told in direct first-person narration, but the story belongs to Leggatt—it is his conundrum that drives the plot. For all the Captain's maneuvering to protect Leggatt, the Captain is not the doer of this story, but the teller, and as he relates to us, the readers, Leggatt's story and the Captain's own complex psychological reaction to it, a similar bond is formed between narrator and reader as was formed between the two characters in the tale.

Heart of Darkness multiplies this implied morality of narration, if we may call it that, many times over. Indeed, it is a frequently noted characteristic of *Heart of Darkness* that we have to do significant analysis just to determine what the story actually is, and who is actually telling it. The telling begins, as it were, on the deck of the cruising yawl *Nellie**, where four friends who were once men of the sea and who still enjoy sailing together are waiting at the head of the Thames for the tide to turn. The reader is addressed by an unnamed narrator, who sets up the situation before Marlow starts to speak. Everything that Marlow will say will come to us through this other narrator whose name we never learn.

So we can fairly easily see a three-layered narrative structure that goes from Marlow, to his companion, to us. But is this really Marlow's story? Or is he not in a similar role in relation to the real story here as the Captain is in *The Secret Sharer*? This is Marlow's story of *hearing* a story.

*Conrad had a friend who had a yawl (a two-sailed boat of yacht size similar to a sloop or cutter, but with a small third mast far aft, near the rudder) named *Nellie*, and thus came the name he used in his novella. However it is also worth noting, an irony of literary history, that the only other significant novel in English preceding *Heart of Darkness* with the same configuration of distancing narrators is *Wuthering Heights*, and the central narrating figure in that story, the equivalent of Marlow, is the maid, whose name is Nellie.

Conrad was by all reports a man who was uncomfortable in society, awkward, shy, and gloomy. Later biographers have revealed that he was subject to fits of temper that led him to be abusive to his family. He never lost his thick accent, although he had done the heretofore unimaginable feat of being a foreigner certified as a captain in the British Merchant Service. It is not clear why he chose, among his five or six languages, to write in the one he learned latest in life: English.

This drama of language and culture and belonging also has its play in *Heart of Darkness*. You'll recall that Conrad goes across to "the Continent," to "the sepulchral city" to gain employment, with the help of his aunt. The city in question is Brussels, and the country is Belgium, which controlled (with unparalleled brutality and savage looting) the entire Congo region. These facts indicate a powerful atmospheric and literary situation that Conrad never once makes explicit: that Marlow, an Englishman, has spent this entire story, until he reaches Kurtz, among French speakers. In addition to the other narrative complications we've explored, we must add the fact that the story has been "translated" by Marlow from French into English, that it took place, as it were, in French. And when Marlow considers why Kurtz has bestowed on him all Kurtz's horrible visions, he concludes that it was "because [he] could speak English to me." So the painful, ruinous, almost lethal redemption that Marlow implicitly claims for himself—having undergone something like Kurtz's own trials and lived to tell of them—resides not only in the successful conveying—the honest evocation—of the story, but in the English language itself. Knowing as we do the facts of Conrad's life—his parents' early deaths after imprisonment by the Russians; his travels; his time on the sea—there is something very moving about his profound connection to the English language, to his commitment to it as a vehicle of redemption, even for

Kurtz, who, having finally found an English speaker, is freed to tell his horrifying truth.

Speech, indeed, is a specific and timely savior. When Marlow rises at midnight and discovers that Kurtz has left the ship, and finds him in the tall grass trying to return to the tribesmen who are loyal to him, Marlow succeeds in stopping him by saying, " 'You will be lost . . . utterly lost' ":

> One gets sometimes such a flash of inspiration, you know. I did say the right thing, though indeed he could not have been more irretrievably lost than he was at this very moment, when the foundations of our intimacy were being laid—to endure—to endure—even to the end—even beyond.

That this unlikely intimacy would endure, long past Kurtz's death, and transform Marlow, becomes the reason why he tells the story to others—each new listener presumably influenced by his own sense of intimacy with Marlow and with his own capacity to change. The story Marlow "hears" is Kurtz's story. Marlow never really tells us what that story is:

> I've been telling you what we said—repeating the phrases we pronounced—but what's the good? They were common everyday words—the familiar, vague sounds exchanged in every waking day of life. But what of that? They had behind them, to my mind, the terrific suggestiveness of words heard in dreams, of phrases spoken in nightmares.

The story resides in the end "at the heart of an impenetrable darkness." The story is all of Europe at its most corrupt. The story is the ruination of a once-fine (though highly mistaken) European intellect; it is the absolute debasement of a self-serving high-mindedness. The story is brutality and madness on a scale and of a depth even greater than what a nineteenth-century

Englishman would attribute to a shaman wearing antelope horns and dancing around a fire. The story is the savagery not of "the savages" but the savagery that Marlow discovers (and that Conrad himself discovered in the Congo, a life-altering experience that helped make him into writer) hidden in the darkness inside each of us, our original and most human inheritance. Most of all, for Conrad, the story is the moral achievement, amid all that debasement and violence and terror, residing in Kurtz's peculiar ability to *convey* all of this, all of the madness and lust and savagery. By being able to speak it, to show it, he is somehow redeemed: he is "a remarkable man."

That is the "story" of *Heart of Darkness* and you really don't get to it until the very end. Indeed, we journey toward it in a structural way—from the *Nellie* to Marlow to Kurtz—that is almost miraculously mirrored in the structure of the story itself, which travels from Europe up the Congo River, stopping at the Outer Station, the Middle Station and the Inner Station, where we find Kurtz, and ivory in unimaginable quantities, and destruction, and speech.

—Vince Passaro

Selected Bibliography

WORKS BY JOSEPH CONRAD

Almayer's Folly: A Story of an Eastern River, 1895 Novel

An Outcast of the Islands, 1896 Novel

The Nigger of the "Narcissus": A Tale of the Sea, 1897 Novel

Tales of Unrest ("Karain: A Memory," "The Idiots," "An Outpost of Progress," "The Return," and "The Lagoon"), 1898 Short Stories

Lord Jim: A Tale, 1900 Novel

The Inheritors: An Extravagant Story (with Ford Madox Hueffer), 1901 Novel

Youth: A Narrative; and Two Other Stories ("Youth," "Heart of Darkness," and "The End of the Tether"), 1902 Novel

Typhoon and Other Stories ("Typhoon," "Amy Foster," "Falk," and "To-morrow"), 1903 Short Stories

Romance: A Novel, 1903 Novel

Nostromo: A Tale of the Seaboard, 1904 Novel

The Mirror of the Sea: Memories and Impressions, 1906 Travel Writings

The Secret Agent: A Simple Tale, 1907 Novel

A Set of Six ("Gaspar Ruiz," "The Informer," "The Brute," "An Anarchist," "The Duel," and "Il Conde"), 1908 Short Stories

Under Western Eyes, 1911 Novel

A Personal Record, 1912 Autobiography

'Twixt Land and Sea: Tales ("A Smile of Fortune," "The Secret Sharer," and "Freya of the Seven Isles"), 1912 Short Stories

Chance: A Tale in Two Parts, 1913 Novel

Within the Tides ("The Planter of Malata," "The Partner," "The Inn of the Two Witches," and "Because of the Dollars"), 1915 Short Stories

Victory: An Island Tale, 1915 Novel

The Shadow-Line, 1917 Novel

The Arrow of Gold: A Story Between Two Notes, 1919 Novel

Notes on Life and Letters, 1921 Memoir

The Rover, 1923 Novel

The Nature of a Crime (with Ford Madox Ford [né Hueffer]), 1924 Novel

Suspense: A Napoleonic Novel (incomplete), 1925 Novel

Tales of Hearsay ("The Warrior's Soul," "Prince Roman," "The Tale," and "The Black Mate"), 1925 Short Stories

Last Essays, 1926 Essays

The Sisters (begun 1896, incomplete), 1928 Novel

Three Plays: Laughing Anne, One Day More, and *The Secret Agent*, 1934 Plays

Congo Diary and Other Uncollected Pieces, 1978 Travel Writings

Criticism and Biography

Batchelor, John. *The Life of Joseph Conrad: A Critical Biography*. Oxford: Blackwell, 1994.

Billy, Ted, ed. *Critical Essays on Joseph Conrad*. Boston: G. K. Hall, 1987.

Bloom, Harold, ed. *Joseph Conrad: Modern Critical Views*. New York: Chelsea House, 1986.

Bode, Rita. " 'They . . . Should Be Out of It': The Women of *Heart of Darkness*." *Conradiana: A Journal of Joseph Conrad Studies* 26:1 (1994), 20–34.

Burden, Robert. *Heart of Darkness*. The Critics Debate Series. Basingstoke: Macmillan, 1991.

Conroy, Mark. *Modernism and Authority: Strategies of Legitimation in Flaubert and Conrad*. Baltimore: Johns Hopkins University Press, 1985.

Greaney, Michael. *Conrad, Language, and Narrative*. Cambridge: Cambridge University Press, 2002.

Hamner, Robert D., ed. *Joseph Conrad: Third World Perspectives*. Washington, DC: Three Continents, 1990.

Hawthorn, Jeremy. *Joseph Conrad: Narrative Technique and Ideological Commitment*. London: Edward Arnold, 1990.

————. *Sexuality and the Erotic in the Fiction of Joseph Conrad*. London: Continuum, 2007.

Henricksen, Bruce. *Nomadic Voices: Conrad and the Subject of Narrative*. Urbana: University of Illinois Press, 1992.

Jameson, Fredric. *The Political Unconscious: Narrative as a Socially Symbolic Act*. London: Methuen; Ithaca, NY: Cornell University Press, 1981.

Knowles, Owen, and Gene M. Moore. *The Oxford Reader's Companion to Joseph Conrad*. Oxford: Oxford University Press, 2000.

Moore, Gene, ed. *Conrad's Cities: Essays for Hans van Marle*. Amsterdam: Rodopi, 1992.

Myers, Jeffrey. *Joseph Conrad: A Biography*. New York: Cooper Square Press, 2001.

Najder, Zdzislaw. *Joseph Conrad: A Chronicle*. Trans. Halina Carroll-Najder. New Brunswick, NJ: Rutgers University Press; Cambridge: Cambridge University Press, 1983.

Parry, Benita. *Conrad and Imperialism: Ideological Boundaries and Visionary Frontiers*. London: Macmillan: Topsfield, MA: Salem Academy/Merrimack, 1984.

Said, Edward W. *Joseph Conrad and the Fiction of Autobiography*. Cambridge, MA: Harvard University Press, 1966.

Stape, J. H., ed. *The Cambridge Companion to Joseph Conrad*. Cambridge: Cambridge University Press, 1966.

———. *The Several Lives of Joseph Conrad*. New York: Pantheon, 2008.

Watt, Ian. *Essays on Conrad*. Cambridge: Cambridge University Press, 2000.

Watts, Cedric. *Joseph Conrad: A Literary Life*. London: Macmillan, 1989.

Classic Fiction

LORD JIM
Joseph Conrad

Tortured by his conscience, an arrogant Englishman flees civilization for a distant jungle trading post. Here, alone in a world which few white men visit, a world where he is worshiped by natives, he begins to discover who he really is.

THE SECRET AGENT
Joseph Conrad

This extraordinary novel is one of Conrad's supreme masterpieces and one of the unquestioned classics of the English novel. It tells a chillingly prophetic tale of terrorism and intrigue, and is a precursor to the espionage thrillers of Graham Greene and John le Carré.

DEATH IN VENICE & Other Stories
Thomas Mann

A wonderful new translation of Mann's masterpiece, this is the tragic story of a foolish, forbidden love, the imagined perfection of youth, and the ruin brought about by an obsessive devotion to "the ideal." This volume includes seven other short stories by Mann.

THE RED BADGE OF COURAGE & Four Stories
Stephen Crane

One of the best known war stories of all time, it captures all the emotions of a young man encountering for the first time the horrors of battle. Originally published in 1895, it was immediately acclaimed by Civil War veterans for its vivid and authentic portrayal. This collection also includes four of Crane's best-known stories.

Available wherever books are sold or at
signetclassics.com

From the
American Renaissance

BILLY BUDD *& Other Tales*
Herman Melville
Collected here are Melville's greatest stories, wry and insightful, or tragic and moving. They are some of the most vivid writing in literature.

TWO YEARS BEFORE THE MAST
Richard Henry Dana, Jr.
One of the most engaging recreations of life at sea ever published. In 1834, Dana signed on as a common seaman for a perilous voyage to California. This is his record of the joys and hardships of a sailor's life. The enormously successful result is both a protest against brutal working conditions and a powerful portrayal of courage and endurance.

LEAVES OF GRASS
Walt Whitman
Here are the incomparable poems of one of America's greatest poets—singer, thinker, visionary, and citizen extraordinaire. Henry David Thoreau said of him, "probably the greatest democrat that ever lived." This newly typeset edition is Whitman's final authorized and complete version of his work.

THE SCARLET LETTER
Nathaniel Hawthorne
Hawthorne's masterpiece is a tale of deceit, adultery, shame and redemption. It provides a tremendously moving insight into the passions of the human heart, and the power of the human psyche.

Available wherever books are sold or at
signetclassics.com

READ THE TOP 20
SIGNET CLASSICS

ANIMAL FARM BY GEORGE ORWELL

1984 BY GEORGE ORWELL

NARRATIVE OF THE LIFE OF FREDERICK DOUGLASS
   BY FREDERICK DOUGLASS

BEOWULF (BURTON RAFFEL, TRANSLATOR)

FRANKENSTEIN BY MARY SHELLEY

ALICE'S ADVENTURES IN WONDERLAND &
   THROUGH THE LOOKING GLASS BY LEWIS CARROLL

THE INFERNO BY DANTE

COMMON SENSE, RIGHTS OF MAN, AND OTHER
   ESSENTIAL WRITINGS BY THOMAS PAINE

HAMLET BY WILLIAM SHAKESPEARE

A TALE OF TWO CITIES BY CHARLES DICKENS

THE HUNCHBACK OF NOTRE DAME BY VICTOR HUGO

THE FEDERALIST PAPERS BY ALEXANDER HAMILTON

THE SCARLET LETTER BY NATHANIEL HAWTHORNE

DRACULA BY BRAM STOKER

THE HOUND OF THE BASKERVILLES
   BY SIR ARTHUR CONAN DOYLE

WUTHERING HEIGHTS BY EMILY BRONTË

THE ODYSSEY BY HOMER

A MIDSUMMER NIGHT'S DREAM BY WILLIAM SHAKESPEARE

FRANKENSTEIN; DRACULA; DR. JEKYLL AND MR. HYDE
   BY MARY SHELLEY, BRAM STOKER, AND ROBERT LOUIS STEVENSON

THE CLASSIC SLAVE NARRATIVES
   EDITED BY HENRY LOUIS GATES, JR.

SIGNETCLASSICS.COM